THE NEW ENGLAND NET

Michael Elia

Text copyright © Michael Elia 2022
Design copyright © Rebeckah Griffiths 2022
All rights reserved.

Michael Elia has asserted his right under the Copyright, Designs and Patents Act 1988 to be identified as the author of this work.

No part of this book may be reprinted or reproduced or utilised in any form or by electronic, mechanical or any other means, now known or hereafter invented, including photocopying or recording, or in any information storage or retrieval system, without the permission in writing from the Publisher and Author.

First published 2022
by Rowanvale Books Ltd
The Gate
Keppoch Street
Roath
Cardiff
CF24 3JW
www.rowanvalebooks.com

A CIP catalogue record for this book is available from the British Library.

Paperback ISBN: 978-1-913662-68-4
eBook ISBN: 978-1-913662-69-1

Part 1

The traffic hurried through the center of Timlook and the noise and exhaust fumes ascended through the air, shaking the foundations of the surrounding buildings.

The police department overlooked the street, and waiting in a truck just outside were eighteen casually dressed mobsters armed with powerful high-velocity rifles, led by a man with long, blond hair and designer stubble, a guy with short, dark hair and piercing eyes, and another dark-haired man with a thick mustache and cold, sinister eyes. These three men, named Sean Radeski, Keith Bergman and Patrick Pilski, were sitting in the vehicle's front seats. The hardened thugs positioned in the main compartment included a reddish-blonde woman, a woman with pure blonde hair, a slightly-built man of thirty-two with short, dark hair, plus a young Pole with fair hair. Sitting in the same row of seats was a fifty-year-old man with medium-length, gray hair, and a rugged, stone-faced guy with shoulder-length blond hair who was thirty-seven. Both were nearly six feet tall with wiry muscles. In the row of seats opposite was a tall, powerfully muscled man of thirty-three with long blond hair, a thinner guy aged thirty-two with long, black hair tied back in a ponytail, a man of forty-four with short, dark hair, a big, stocky black man who was mustached, and five other young men including a sharp-eyed youth of twenty-three with blond hair. Sat on the floor of the main compartment were a bearded guy with long, black hair and a man of thirty-four who was tall and strongly muscled, with long, wavy blond hair. They waited for ten minutes before Sean Radeski addressed Keith Bergman and Patrick Pilski.

"It's lunch break but the cops are not coming outside the department!" he snapped violently. "We must go inside and massacre the bastards!"

"You're a guy who's ruthless when taking risks, but that would be bloody reckless," Bergman added coolly. "It will be a messy operation if the cops retaliate."

"You're telling me, Keith," Pilski agreed, his smile sinister, his voice slow and cold. "But we can't hang about here any longer."

"In that case, I'm in if everybody else is," Bergman remarked.

"Right guys, we make our move, leave no survivors, and then we get out," Radeski snarled. "We must target Dave Bradley, James Mitchell and Melissa Morgan. Our boss has an old score to settle with those three, a score that's lasted nine years. Are we all in?"

"It looks like we have an accord." Bergman laughed, and then all three mobsters thrust their balaclavas over their faces.

Seizing their rifles, they climbed outside, hurried to the rear and opened the back doors. Everybody jumped out, fully armed, and advanced towards the police department's entrance. They climbed the steps and moved with determined speed through the corridor. Nine uniformed cops were heading towards them from the main office door and panicked on spotting the three masked ringleaders leading the fearsome mob. The cops reached for their handguns. Radeski, Bergman and Pilski aimed their rifles, squeezed the triggers and vomited eight, savage, ear-bursting shots into three of the uniforms, sending them hurtling to the stone floor, blood gushing from their wounds. The fair-haired Pole, the two women and the dark-haired, slightly-built guy blazed many times with their own rifles, while the blond, muscular man, the dark guy with the ponytail and the middle-aged man with short, dark hair pumped three spurts of rifle fire towards them. All nine cops went down in just a few seconds. There was panic amongst the mob leaders.

"Fuck this, man, we've blown it!" Radeski yelled.

"We've lost the element of surprise!" Pilski shouted.

"It's now or never, let's frigging move, go, go, go!" Bergman cried, his voice vicious. The mobsters charged towards the door of the main office.

***

Having heard the gunfire in the corridor, Detectives Dave Bradley, James Mitchell and Nicole Lamenski yanked their handguns out of their holsters. Dale Manuchi and Melissa Morgan followed suit, followed by Captain Robert Merson, John Reynolds and Bernardo Ruiz. Vice Squad

Leader Richard Kanaris grabbed a rifle as the other bearded vice cops Jan Muller, John Felt and Matt Felder seized their rifles too, and a blond, mustached guy named Mark Blondel pulled a .45 Magnum out of his leather jacket.

Merson and the homicide detectives dived behind their desks in the nick of time, but Kanaris's men were too late. Radeski's thugs hurried through the entrance door and into the main office, and Radeski and Bergman pumped five ferocious gunshots towards Kanaris and Muller, while the strongly muscled blond guy, the dark-haired man with the ponytail, and the middle-aged dark guy blazed with vicious savagery towards Felt, Felder and Blondel. Luckily, the vice cops were wearing bullet-proof vests, for no sooner than they had raised their weaponry to retaliate, they fell violently to the floor, the rifle bullets only penetrating their vests and puncturing their chests enough to immobilize them.

Radeski, Bergman, Pilski and the eighteen mobsters pressed home their fierce barrage of rifle fire and sent a terrifying hail of large, fiery-hot bullets, bombarding the walls, windows, desks and the Captain's office in a merciless assault to kill Dave's people and leave no survivors. But the desks were made of thick wood and metal and absorbed the bullets. Before long, the mobsters had run out of ammunition and reached into their leather jackets to reload.

"Now!" Dave screamed.

Popping up from behind their desks, Merson, Dave, Jim and the others focused their handguns and blasted with terrible ferocity, vomiting a barrage of deafening shots which rang out through the office. Jim brought down the big, mustached black guy and the sharp-eyed youth with eight shots, while Dave and Dale each cut down two of the remaining four youths with a total of fifteen blasts. Nicole sent seven shots into the reddish-blonde woman and the fair-haired Pole just as Melissa blasted the other blonde woman and the slightly-built, dark-haired man with a total of eight fierce shots. Reynolds, Bernardo and Captain Merson were also firing savagely, their vicious volley of fifteen bullets cutting through the powerfully muscled blond guy, the man with the ponytail and the middle-aged thug with dark hair. The thugs hurtled to the floor in rivers of blood, leaving only Radeski, Bergman and Pilski, plus the dark-haired, bearded guy, the man with wavy blond hair, the gray-haired man, and the stony-faced guy with long blond hair.

Having reloaded their rifles, the thugs fired another ferocious barrage of burning ammo towards Dave, Jim and Dale, who crawled along the floor behind their desks, terror shaking and numbing their nerves as their teeth clenched.

Then, Nicole fired four bullets towards the mobsters and Jim sent another five rounds blazing from his automatic revolver, but both Dave's partners missed. Captain Merson and Melissa darted up from behind their desks and blazed with deadly violence, Merson killing the gray-haired man with six lethal shots, while Melissa got the blond, stone-faced guy with five rounds.

Reynolds, Bernardo and Jim fired repeatedly at the mob leaders, but Radeski, Bergman and Pilski retreated through the office door and fled down the corridor. The strongly muscled guy with wavy hair and the bearded killer covered the leaders' escape by blasting towards Jim, Reynolds and Bernardo, then at Melissa and Captain Merson, for a terrifying period of ten seconds. This interval worked to the advantage of Dave and Dale. The young detectives jumped up above their desks, aimed their revolvers with ruthless accuracy and pumped nine deafening shots into the two men, Dave dispatching the wavy-haired guy with five blasts, while Dale accounted for the bearded man with another four rounds. Both thugs were sprawled awkwardly across the office floor. All eighteen men and women lay in their own carnage, the corpses creating pools of blood, staining the office floor dark red.

"Are you okay, Captain?" Dave asked frantically.

"Yeah, I'm okay!" Merson replied.

"The masked men are getting away!" Nicole cried.

"We'll go after them! Dave, Nicole, come with me!" Jim ordered.

Having reloaded their handguns, Dave, Jim and Nicole ran towards the door and sped down the corridor leading to the steps that descended onto the street, covering the distance in eight seconds. They saw the masked men career the truck onto the main street and then accelerate westwards towards the outskirts of Timlook. Dave and Jim wasted no time in pulling open the squad van's doors and leaping into the front seats, while Nicole yanked open the back doors and hurried into one of the two rows of seats positioned on either side, sat down and slammed the doors shut. As Dave and Jim fastened their seatbelts, Jim thrust his keys into the ignition and accelerated down the street. The van lurched and sped at fifty miles per hour as Jim pursued the truck. As Nicole tried to secure her seatbelt, she was thrown about, but eventually managed to fasten it tightly against her wiry body.

"Watch your speed, Jim!" Nicole yelled. "Or I'll fly through the window!"

"Listen here, Nicole, three thugs are getting away and I can't lose them!" Jim snapped. "So you can put a stop to your complaints!"

"Watch the road, Jim!" Dave ordered. "The last thing we need is dead pedestrians making a mess of our squad van! The truck is heading towards the western suburbs of Timlook. We'll need back-up in case the masked men have more of their guys at the other end waiting for us!"

"Use the walkie-talkie, kid!" Jim suggested.

Dave pressed the On/Off button of the walkie-talkie.

"Calling all units, calling all units, an army truck is cutting down the main street towards the western outskirts of Timlook. The truck is leaving the city and driving towards a massive field with an airstrip, near the forest. Three masked men are driving the vehicle, they are armed and highly dangerous. There may be more armed men on the field. Over and out."

"There are more of them," Jim muttered.

"How many of these guys?" Nicole asked.

"Too many," Dave replied. "And they have a transport plane with them."

"These are not ex-cons or petty criminals with a grudge against us," Jim snarled. "Otherwise, how come they have enough bucks to own a plane?"

"You're right, Jim," Dave agreed. "These are a syndicate of organized criminals. Arms or drug dealers."

"They're turning down the lane onto the airstrip on the field," Jim growled. "I'm about to turn in and get as close to the plane as possible. Then we'll hide behind the van."

"And engage these bastards in a shootout," Dave said.

The squad van was five hundred yards behind as the truck came to within thirty yards of the plane, doubled back and ground to a halt with its rear to the plane and its front facing the van. Radeski, Bergman and Pilski scrambled out of the front, pulled back their balaclavas and joined their back-up gang of mobsters waiting by the plane. There were three ex-marines in suits and a powerfully built, rough-tough guy with long, brown hair growing down either side of a bald patch on his head and dressed in jeans and a denim shirt. The marines were a gray-haired man in his fifties named Nick Sommers, a blond guy with a thick mustache and sunglasses, and a black guy with a sinister face and leering grin. The casual, rough-looking man was a Pole, and he greeted Radeski, Bergman and Pilski before they all hurried into the plane, along with the three ex-marines. Radeski climbed into the cockpit and started the plane's engine.

To cover the men's escape as their plane advanced down the airstrip, a casually dressed gang of eight mobsters, namely three bearded Mexicans and five Americans, four of the Americans being dark-haired with army-style haircuts and the fifth being fair-haired, focused their rifles on Jim's squad van.

Struck with terror at the intimidating sight, Jim swerved the van round to a right angle before the detectives dropped their heads down. Jim switched off the ignition, then he and Dave scrambled across the driver's seat on the far side of the van, opened the door and leapt outside. Nicole kicked open the back doors, jumped out and crawled underneath the van to avoid the rifle fire, joining Dave and Jim on the sheltered side.

The mobsters showered the van with a ferocious bombardment of rifle fire, the lethal hail of bullets smashing all the windows and denting the metalwork.

Dave and Jim knew it was impossible to retaliate from where they were as the eight thugs had pinned them behind the van, giving them no chance to fire back. But then the three detectives crawled underneath the bonnet. Broken glass fell behind them as they pulled themselves through the confined space between the van's four wheels. They overcame their fear like army commandos enduring an assault course. When they reached the other side underneath the vehicle, they aimed their handguns and blazed without mercy. Nicole fired six shots before her gun ran out of ammunition. Dave sent two shots into one of the Americans, then three into another, just as Jim fired two shots into the fair-haired thug, three into another dark-haired guy and then three more into the last gunman, the bullets bloodying the men's chests.

These Americans had been extremely dangerous, highly trained gunmen who had nearly killed the detectives with their lethal shower of rifle fire, but Dave and Jim's well-aimed revolver fire had finished all five men within two terrifying minutes.

The bearded Mexicans blasted towards Dave and Jim before hurrying into their truck's front seats and driving the heavy vehicle towards the squad van, ready to ram it out of the way and ruthlessly drive over Dave, Jim and Nicole.

Originally, the plane was going to ram the van and drive savagely over the detectives, but this would have broken the propellor blades in front as they would not have been strong enough to slice and hack through the van without breaking off, immobilizing the aircraft and destroying the dealers' chance of escaping from Pennsylvania. Instead, Sean Radeski's plane had skidded round them on the airstrip, driven down the length of grass and then ascended into the air, towards Detroit.

Dave and Jim would never nail Sean Radeski and Nick Sommers now, but there was still the truck.

Scrambling to their feet from under the bonnet, Dave, Jim and Nicole, having already reloaded their revolvers, aimed the lethal handguns at the oncoming truck's windshield. The vehicle sped towards them, closing the distance to forty yards, then thirty yards and then twenty.

"Stop, or we'll fire!" Jim yelled, but his warning failed to intimidate the three Mexicans seated in front.

Nicole was the first detective to open fire, blasting five savage gunshots into the driver, all of them hitting bang on target. The bullets penetrated the windshield and slammed viciously into the driver's chest so that he slumped onto the steering wheel. Dave blasted the second guy with six shots, and the brute was thrown back into his seat. Jim blazed with six gunshots into the man who had headed the eight-strong gang of Mexicans and Americans, and the mob leader fell hard against the passenger side door. Then the detectives dodged as the truck turned and crashed into the fence closing off the field and airstrip from the highway.

"Damn you, you arseholes," Jim muttered. He quickly turned round and faced Dave and Nicole. "Two of those three masked men, plus the balding man with long hair and those three ex-marines in suits were Sean Radeski's thugs. The man with long, blond hair and an unshaven face was Radeski himself. The guy with short, dark hair who was clean-shaven was Keith Bergman, and the evil-looking psycho with short, dark hair, cold eyes and a thick mustache was Patrick Pilski. I know about the bald guy, the mustached bloke with sunglasses and the black guy, and the grey-haired man was Nick Sommers. All four Poles and three ex-marines make up Sean Radeski's drug cartel in Detroit. The other five Americans and three bearded Mexicans were from Jose Cortez's drug cartel in New York, and as you've seen just now, both gangs of thugs were extremely violent and highly dangerous men who knew what they were doing.

"Radeski's mobsters have slipped through our fingers this time and will no doubt make another attempt to put us all in the ground."

"And even worse, those thugs we killed were only the tip of the iceberg," Dave added. "Jose Cortez has a whole mob in his New York cartel to replace the men we gunned down. The eighteen who attacked Timlook PD almost massacred us. They were highly trained professionals and obviously had a deadly score to settle. We've had a hell of a fight to defeat those eighteen men and women plus the eight thugs covering Radeski's escape, but it's only the beginning of our nightmare. We're right back to square one. And we're still up against two drug cartels in Detroit and New York, plus two more in Chicago and Boston.

"And even worse, the cartel in Chicago is run by Matt and Ray Mck-Fee, who were recently released from Illinois's maximum-security prison. The Mck-Fees are younger brothers of James Mck-Fee whom Melissa shot and killed at the Metaxes Saloon in Athens Street in August 2000. Melissa saved my life as he was about to kill me. Together, we smashed the Jingles and Mck-Fee cartels.

"I have a hunch that a network of drug cartels want us three, Melissa and the rest of Timlook PD six feet underground. Matt and Ray Mck-Fee want us dead for Melissa's killing of their elder brother, and as the new Mck-Fee Drug Cartel in Chicago plays a big part in the network of cartels between Chicago and the east coast, they are probably the top cartel in this ruthless narcotics ring.

"But this is only speculation on my part. We must collect the dead gunmen's DNA samples, run a check on the department's DNA database and figure out whether there's a connection between these mobsters, Sean Radeski's guys and the Mck-Fees. And then us three, Dale and Melissa plus Reynolds and Bernardo must find the dealers before they find us."

"The drug cartels in Chicago, Detroit, New York and Boston were fighting each other, sending hitmen to kill one another's drug lords and stealing millions of dollars' worth of arms, drugs and money," Nicole said. "But now they have stopped fighting each other and united under the Mck-Fees to combat American law enforcement, which means we have a major war on our hands."

"A war that can never be won," Dave replied.

"Wiping out eighteen of Sean Radeski's people and eight of Jose Cortez's thugs won't solve the problem we're facing now," Jim growled.

"I see a squad of uniforms driving towards us with the Forensics and CSI teams," Nicole said.

Five squad cars carrying uniformed cops, plus another five vehicles occupied by the Forensics and CSI people came down the highway and turned into the field before advancing towards Dave, Jim and Nicole. The men and women left the vehicles and approached the detectives.

"Where the hell were you guys when we needed you?" Dave inquired, his voice aggressive.

The uniforms and the CSI and Forensics people were horrified by the carnage of dead mobsters and beaten-up trucks.

***

After the Forensics and CSI teams had removed the bodies of Cortez's mobsters from the field and Radeski's people from the carnage at Timlook PD's main office, Dave, Jim and Nicole visited Richard Kanaris's vice cops at Tefflin Hospital. The bearded hippy detectives were grateful they had been wearing their bullet-proof vests when Radeski's thugs gunned them down; they had only suffered minor wounds to their chests and their conditions were stable. Having recovered, the vice cops would return to the department the next day.

Dave, Jim and Nicole left the hospital and drove towards the department. They parked the van outside the building, where a mass of reporters were grilling Captain Robert Merson about the shootout. They shoved their way through the crowd, entered the building and walked down the corridor. Making their way into the main office, they encountered the Forensics and CSI teams combing every square foot of the vast room. The CSI inspector approached them.

"You can't come in here," the inspector told them.

"It's okay, we work here," Dave explained.

"We're the police," Jim informed him. "Dave, Nicole, show the inspector your badges and ID."

"Here we go," Dave said lightly. "I'm Detective Dave Bradley. We're Homicide Detectives."

"I'm Detective Nicole Lamenski," Nicole added. "I'm Dave's wife and also Dave and Jim's partner in operations."

"I'm Detective Sergeant James Mitchell," Jim explained. "I am Head of Homicide and I answer only to Captain Merson. You know where Detectives Dale Manuchi, Melissa Morgan, John Reynolds and Bernardo Ruiz are?"

"In the computer room running DNA checks on the twenty-six mob guys the eight of you brought down single-handed," the inspector replied. "This place resembles a bomb site. It must've been the shootout to end all shootouts. And the eight of you took on the whole mob and killed all twenty-six without any of you catching a bullet. The odds were just over three to one."

"Nine uniforms were killed, and five vice cops were wounded, but their vests saved them," Dave informed him. "We've just come back from paying them a visit at Tefflin Hospital, and they've recovered."

"I'm sorry about the nine uniforms," the inspector said. "But I'm glad Kanaris's vice cops are okay. Have the uniforms' families been informed?"

"Yeah, they've been informed," Nicole said. "The twenty-six hardmen were all members of two drugs cartels based in Detroit and New York."

"Okay, let's cut to the chase," Jim started. "Three men in balaclavas, who were leading the mobsters, escaped from us when they got onto a plane with a bald man and three ex-marines.

"The marines were kicked out of the military in 2005 for selling hard drugs to fellow marines traumatized by their battle experiences in Iraq. Their twenty-one victims believed dope would take the pressure off and make them feel like they were on top of the world, but nine died and twelve are still going cold turkey. Three dealers: a clean-shaven black man, a blond man with a mustache, and the ringleader, a gray-haired man in his fifties named Nick Sommers, were caught, tried and court-marshaled. The three ex-marines started working for Sean Radeski's drug cartel in Detroit.

"When the three masked men removed their balaclavas, we saw their faces. They were Sean Radeski, Keith Bergman and Patrick Pilski, all Poles. The casually dressed guy with long, brown hair and a bald patch was also a Pole, and all four casually dressed thugs plus the three ex-marines got onto the plane and took off from the field. That was the Detroit drug cartel. The five Americans with army haircuts and the three bearded Mexicans who covered the escape were working for Jose Cortez's Mexican drug cartel in New York."

"How do you know all this?" the Inspector asked Jim.

"It was here in Timlook that the ex-marines were court-marshaled then bailed out by Radeski, Bergman, Pilski and the bald Pole," Jim pointed out. "The Poles hired the ex-marines as new recruits before fleeing to Detroit where the cartel is based.

"The five Americans and three bearded Mexicans were arms dealers supplying weapons from Timlook to Jose Cortez's cartel in New York, but when they were caught and tried, Cortez bailed them out, hired all eight of them, and they escaped with Cortez to New York and disappeared somewhere in the Big Apple.

"Both cartels escaped justice because Sean Radeski and Jose Cortez paid dirty cops in Timlook, Detroit and New York to destroy the evidence against Nick Sommers's guys, the five Americans and three Mexicans."

"Except that now, all eight men working for Cortez finally got their Vietnam when myself, Jim and Nicole pumped lead into them at the airfield," Dave explained. "Both drug cartels have stopped fighting a rival gang war with two cartels in Chicago and Boston, and all four have formed an alliance to fight American law enforcement. We suspect that the Chicago cartel is the top cartel, headed by the Mck-Fee brothers, Matt and Ray."

"Their brother, James Mck-Fee, ran a cartel here in Timlook before in August of 2000, Dave, Jim and Melissa smashed the Mck-Fee Cartel by defeating its members in a shootout in a car park in Athens Street," Nicole added.

"I chased James Mck-Fee into the Metaxes Saloon where we had a punch-up, Mck-Fee aimed a piece at me and Melissa saved my life," Dave explained. "A month later, his two younger brothers, Matt and Ray, were arrested in Chicago, tried and sentenced to fifteen years detention in Illinois's maximum-security prison. They served less than nine years, were released in March 2009, and formed a new drug cartel in Chicago.

"The judge phoned Timlook PD and warned us that the Mck-Fees would put out a hit on me, Jim and Melissa and the rest of Timlook PD. Me and Melissa were terrified. Now it's April 2009, and we've just survived an attempted massacre by two other cartels."

"Neither Radeski nor Cortez bore a grudge against us," Jim growled. "The new Mck-Fee Cartel must have formed a pact with the Radeski and Cortez cartels to have us all killed."

"And now, Dale, Melissa, Reynolds and Bernardo must've finished ferreting through the DNA Database," Dave remarked. "If my theory is wrong… please God, let me be wrong."

"No, Dave, your theory is spot-on," Dale called, sticking his head through the computer room's doorway. "We've finished the DNA check on all twenty-six mob guys."

"We browsed through the Database and traced any possible links to other mobs." Reynolds chuckled.

"And guess what we discovered," Dale said with a laugh.

"Yeah, tell me," Dave demanded.

"The trail led to the new Mck-Fee Cartel in Chicago." Melissa sounded nervous. "I don't like it, Dave, Dale. I gunned down their big brother nine years ago, and now they've put out a hit on me."

"The hit targeted all of us, Melissa." Dale comforted his wife.

She fell against his chest and began trembling as he embraced her.

"Hey, it's okay, my love." He reassured her again. "I'll protect you. We're all here if you need us. Do you want to take a few days off, honey?"

She looked up into his eyes with her mouth agape, her eyes shy and wet.

"I'll be fine, my love," Melissa said. "I mustn't let the team down."

"You never let the team down, honey," Dale said. "You had to kill Mck-Fee to protect Dave. You saved Dave's life."

"None of us could've foreseen the consequences of your actions," Dave told her. "I've never forgotten what you did for me."

"I'm proud of what I did," Melissa stated. "Mck-Fee was an evil man and he had to be stopped. I always knew I would do the same thing again."

"And you did, honey," Dale added. "When you saved my life in my spare house outside Blackrock. Detectives Jack Doogan and Rick Baxter and six other dirty cops tried to kill us. During that fight, we gunned down three of them. I was shot and came close to death, but your bloody-minded skill and determination with first aid saved me. I'll never forget that, just as Dave will never forget how you got Mck-Fee off his back in the Metaxes Saloon."

"You'll be okay, Melissa," Bernardo promised her.

"We're here if you need us," Reynolds said.

"I'll get you a drink," Dave decided.

"Thanks, Dave." Melissa chuckled. "You know how to find your way to a woman's heart."

"It's only water," Jim objected.

"Water suits me," she reassured him.

"I'll get it," Nicole offered.

"I'll get it," Dave insisted. "I'm thirsty myself, so that's two mugs of water. And here comes Captain Merson."

"Have the reporters gone, Captain?" the inspector asked.

"They're still out there," Merson replied, his voice abrupt. "The press is having a field day. We're in the news for all the wrong reasons."

"We follow," Jim said. "They're not called the gutter press for nothing."

Dave made his way to the kitchen flanking the main office. When he re-joined everybody in the computer room, his mind was eager for more information on possible leads other than the Mck-Fees. He passed a mug of water to Melissa.

"Thanks, Dave," she said.

Dale played with Melissa's bunched-up ponytail before squeezing her shoulder, his hand caressing her dark blue sweater.

"That's strong perfume," Dale commented.

"I'll get a milder one next time," Melissa replied.

"I meant it as a compliment," Dale said. "You can't take a compliment."

"I was joking," she said. "I thought men like women with a sense of humor."

"Forgive me, I missed the joke," Dale objected. "I hope the compliment stands."

"You mind concentrating on the case?" Merson demanded.

"Sorry, Captain," Dale replied.

"All these dead mobsters are linked to Cortez, Radeski and the Mck-Fees," Jim informed everybody.

"We must find the Mck-Fees," Dave said. "By making a trip to Chicago and cooperating with Chicago Homicide and the FBI's Illinois branch. We'll go as soon as Kanaris's men return and we pull other uniforms from Timlook's second department and two other departments in Harrisburg and Gettysburg."

"I can arrange that, Bradley," Merson promised.

"Hey, take a look at this!" Jim exclaimed.

"Found something?" Reynolds blurted.

"Another lead?" Bernardo asked.

"You bet," Jim enthused.

"Well, tell us now!" Dale protested.

"Cortez and the Mck-Fees arranged via two phone calls to pull a deal with the Juan Pazerra Cuban drug cartel in Miami, on April twenty-second, 2009," Jim explained. "That was only five days ago." He turned to address Nicole. "The question is, how did Miami PD find out about Cortez and the Mck-Fees phoning Juan Pazerra? What was the deal and why didn't Chief Kavubu or Sam Ringwood's vice squad give you a call soon after to inform us? Can you explain?"

"Your guess is as good as mine," Nicole said.

"They didn't know we had any interest in Cortez or Pazerra, or that the Mck-Fees want us dead," Dale suggested.

"A good guess, Dale," Jim replied. "But wrong answer."

"The information's here," Dave insisted. "Question one: how did Miami PD get wind of the phone call to Pazerra? The answer is, Chicago PD and New York PD had tapped the phones of the Mck-Fees and Cortez, while Miami PD tapped Pazerra's. The Mck-Fees and Cortez exchanged phone calls, then made two calls to Juan Pazerra on April twenty-second and arranged to visit him. But on April twenty-fourth, the Mck-Fees ordered Cortez to head for Florida without them, for the Mck-Fees were arranging eight of Cortez's men and Radeski's guys to pull a hit operation against us, and on April twenty-fifth they attacked us, but we beat them.

"The day before the attack on us, the Mck-Fees decided to stay in Chicago to maintain contact with Radeski's people and keep up to date on how the operation against us went, so, Cortez and two other Mexicans made the helicopter trip on their own and met up with Juan Pazerra's Cuban mobsters on the rooftop of his cartel building in Miami's Little Havana.

"The Miami vice squads under Sam Ringwood and Jack Trogan found out more info, especially on what kind of deal Cortez will pull with Pazerra, by infiltrating the Pazerra Cartel.

"Question two is, what is the deal? And question three is, what is the motive behind it? To begin with, Cortez and Pazerra are close friends in the underworld, and Pazerra turned to Cortez for help. The deal is that Pazerra and a few of his thugs will fly to New York with Cortez to join Cortez's drug cartel. And the motive is that the Miami Police are tightening their net on the Pazerra Cartel, and Pazerra, along with a handful of bodyguards, know their days in Florida are numbered before the Miami Vice Squads bust them and they will face the can. Cortez and Pazerra must've exchanged phone calls before April twenty-second, Pazerra making the first call, offering to join Cortez's mob.

"Cortez's group are probably in Miami now, making the deal with Pazerra's guys.

"And question four is, why didn't Miami PD's Chief Kavubu call Timlook PD, or Sam Ringwood give Nicole a call after discovering this info?"

"Dale answered that question for you," Melissa insisted.

"Because they had no knowledge of our interest in Cortez or Pazerra, or that the drug cartels wanted us dead," Dale repeated.

"And I told Dale that the guess was good, but the answer was wrong," Jim repeated.

"Dale's answer was wrong because Captain Merson's question was wrong," Dave said.

"How do you mean?" Merson wanted to know.

"Sam Ringwood did not phone Nicole, but Miami PD did send us the answer via the Police Internet Database," Dave informed the captain. "They didn't need to phone us directly. Your question was wrong because Miami PD did pass us the info, and it's written down right here in an email. Emails have also been passed to other police departments from Miami to Boston."

"But the email to us was late," Jim added scathingly. "Miami PD only found out that Cortez wanted us dead after Cortez's men worked with Radeski's in that hit against us.

"If Pazerra flees Florida with his thugs and Cortez's gang, Sam Ringwood's vice squad will trail them, take on the Cubans and Mexicans in New York, and capture them dead or alive. Sam will need our help to nail Pazerra, and we'll need Sam's help to nail Cortez.

"On top of all this, our help and Sam's, along with the incriminating information and details of legal negotiations which we can share, are vital to the police departments in Chicago, Detroit and New York in order to bust the Mck-Fee, Radeski and Cortez-Pazerra cartels, prosecute them in their own jurisdictions, convict all the dealers and put them away for life. Sam Ringwood's people will have to join us here in Timlook, hire another squad van, and then both our teams must make that trip to Chicago to find the Mck-Fees. Sam's lawyer son, Toby Ringwood, must come over with the vice cops to negotiate the legal side with the Court of Justice in Chicago and exchange information.

"By targeting the Mck-Fees in Chicago first, we'll be attacking the really big game at the top, namely the main drug cartel behind the hit operation against us, and then we'll work our way down the network by repeating the sequence of police and courtroom operations in Detroit, then New York and then Boston.

"With Sam's people cooperating with us to nail Pazerra and Cortez in New York, Toby can negotiate with the New York Court of Justice to have Pazerra and his thugs extradited to Miami to stand trial for narcotics deals committed in Florida."

"I must give Sam a call and tell him five cartels, including Juan Pazerra's, have a vendetta against us, and that we must combine our police and legal manpower with his vice squad and Toby," Nicole said. "I'll ask them to take the FBI plane to Timlook, so both our teams can cooperate to smash the cartels piece by piece, starting with a trip to Chicago."

"Go ahead," Merson invited her.

She passed through the door, covered the distance across the bullet-ridden office and pushed past the CSI people before making her way into the changing room to grab her phone.

***

In Miami's rough suburb of Little Havana, three mustached Mexicans, including Jose Cortez, landed in a helicopter on the roof of Juan Pazerra's hideout and greeted the bushy-bearded Hispanic who was standing between two other bearded Cubans with long hair and sunglasses. After Cortez turned off the helicopter's engine, all six long-haired men headed through the door leading from the roof, and down some steps to the saloon area, passing several basic rooms on the way. Once inside the saloon, they were surrounded by over two dozen bearded and mustached Cubans sat at scattered tables, all rough-tough hardmen working for Pazerra. Both drug lords and their bodyguards sat down around a table and began pulling the deal, totally unaware that the saloon was bugged.

Waiting outside the building's front entrance were vice cops Jack Trogan, Jim Curry, Bruce Dwane and Enrique Rogers, positioned alongside four other hippy cops. Trogan was in his early forties with short, brown hair, a serious-looking face and a thick mustache. Curry resembled the actor Jeff Bridges, with his medium-length blond hair and beard, just as Dwane was the spitting image of the film star Willem Dafoe, his face rugged, but with long blond hair. Rogers resembled the 1980s pop singer Michael McDonald, with his stocky build, long grey hair and bushy beard. The other four hippy detectives were also bearded and had medium-length hair. The youngest was a small man, aged thirty-seven, with brown hair, followed by a diminutive black man of forty with a small beard and mustache, then a blond guy of forty-two and a brown-haired man of forty-three.

Running up from behind and in front of the hippy detectives were more of Jack Trogan's men and Sam Ringwood's people. The rest of Trogan's vice cops included a dark-haired man with a mustache and glasses, two guys with long blond hair and a bearded man with medium-length, fair hair, plus two mustached Cubans, three bearded men with long hair and sunglasses, and a black man with glasses and a medium-length mustache, all dressed in jeans, T-shirts and leather jackets.

In the second vice squad facing Trogan's were Sam Ringwood, Rico Carrouso and Martin Goldblum stood beside Glen Hawke, Lopez Carreras, a Phil Collins look-alike who was long-haired and unshaven by the name of Philo Magee, and four women named Clara Brown, Christine Milano, Martine Corday and Wendy Molanski.

Waiting inside Sam's squad van, keeping tabs on the bugged conversation between Cortez and Pazerra, were Chief Kavubu and Captain Frank Olmera.

Enrique Rogers whispered back to Trogan, Curry and Dwane, "Pazerra and Cortez are hesitating."

"We'll just wait," Trogan replied.

"This is where it gets interesting," Sam commented.

"Can you hear what these guys are saying?" Magee asked Sam and Carrouso. "Because I can't."

"I can't hear anything," Sam remarked.

"I'm waiting for the go-ahead to attack," Carrouso growled.

"It will come," Goldblum added.

"What are the dealers up to?" Curry whispered.

"I don't know," Rogers replied.

"It sure beats the hell out of me," Dwane retorted.

"What do you make of it, Sam?" Trogan muttered.

"Kavubu and Olmera will bleep us," Sam remarked.

"If we go in, we must do it now," Dwane said. "Before the bird flies out of the cage."

"The dealers are talking again," Rogers told Dwane.

"Let the deal carry through," Magee demanded. "Or we won't have a case."

"We wait too long and we won't capture Pazerra and Cortez," Carrouso snarled. "And Sam, I understand Nicole gave you a call?"

"She did."

"What did she tell you?" Carrouso wanted to know.

"Casual conversation comes later, Rico," Goldblum growled.

"Just briefly," Sam told them. "Our people in Timlook Homicide need our help to nail four drug cartels."

"If we nail Cortez and Pazerra, it will only be three," Trogan said.

"And if we lose them, it'll be five," Dwane added.

"What else did Nicole say?" Curry asked.

"Mobsters from two of the cartels attacked Timlook PD," Sam said. "And they're linked to two black drug dealers called the Mck-Fees."

"The brothers of James Mck-Fee, who Melissa wasted?" Glen asked.

"It sounds familiar," Lopez added.

"And now the Mck-Fees want retribution," Trogan agreed.

"And Dave and Nicole need your help to nail them?" Dwane asked Sam.

"They sure do," Sam replied harshly. "And now, I hear Chief Kavubu and Captain Olmera bleeping me. What is it, Captain?"

"Pazerra, Cortez and their bodyguards are running back upstairs," Olmera told Sam.

"You guys, move in now!" Kavubu ordered.

"Good luck," Olmera said to Sam.

"We'll need it," Sam replied.

"Do we go in?" Trogan asked Sam.

"We go in," Sam confirmed the order. The vice cops smashed open the door and stormed into the saloon, taking the twenty-five Cubans completely by surprise.

"Freeze, Miami Vice!" Carrouso yelled.

"On the floor!" Goldblum screamed.

"Don't try anything funny!" Lopez cried.

"Or we'll fill you with lead!" Clara shouted.

Focusing their handguns, Clara, Christine, Martine and Wendy pushed four Cubans to the floor, restrained and handcuffed them, just as Carrouso, Goldblum, Glen and Lopez forced another four against the wall before cuffing them. The other cops used their rifles to bash the remaining dealers to the floor as Sam and Magee covered the detectives with their own rifles.

"Where are Cortez and Pazerra?" Dwane demanded.

"They're upstairs!" a mobster replied. "With two Mexicans, two Cubans and two Americans!"

"Two Americans!" Trogan yelled.

"Who are these Americans?" Dwane demanded.

"Two new recruits to Pazerra's cartel," the mobster wailed.

"This is something new!" Sam cried.

"They're about to escape in the helicopter!" Curry pointed out, his voice harsh.

"Sam, Curry, Dwane and four other men go upstairs and stop them!" Trogan ordered the other squad leader. "We fail to nail them now and they'll slip through our fingers like fish through a net. The rest of us will stay down here to guard the remaining mobsters."

"I'll go with them," the mustached black cop with glasses volunteered.

"Let's move!" Sam commanded the others. Sam, Curry, Dwane and the black guy pushed open the door and raced upstairs, joined by the mustached white cop with glasses and the three men with long, blond hair, the third guy bearded.

Sam's mustache and designer stubble were irritated by the Florida heat just as Curry's beard and Dwane's rugged face were also itching, but the cool air-conditioning over the steps and in the surrounding rooms was a refreshing relief from the intense warmth outside.

"They must be on the roof!" Dwane shouted.

"They are on the roof!" Curry snarled.

"Head for the roof now!" Sam growled.

All eight cops reached the flat hideout roof in the next six seconds, their rifles ready to fire.

***

On the hideout roof, Cortez, Pazerra and their bodyguards were joined by the two casually-dressed Americans, the first with long brown hair and a beard, the second with long blond hair and an evil, leering face, both mobsters rough-tough killers who enjoyed violence. Pazerra turned to the Americans.

"Gracias, you guys, for tipping me off that the cops were coming," he thanked them.

"The cops are chicken-shit idiots, man," the bearded man sneered.

"We saw the two vice squads through the upstairs window, and then we bleeped you on your mobile to warn you." The blond guy chuckled, his laughter evil and malicious.

"You two Americans can come back to New York with us," Pazerra snarled.

"Get inside the helicopter now," Cortez growled.

The bodyguards pulled open the helicopter's side doors before jumping into the back seats with the Americans. Pazerra and Cortez leapt into the front seats, slammed the doors shut and punched the chopper's ignition. The rotor spun round with deadly speed and the helicopter climbed into the air, glided over the rooftop and hovered away above the white stone buildings of Miami.

***

Sam, Dwane, Curry and the other five cops charged through the rooftop door too late, but they raced across the roof, aimed their rifles and fired towards the helicopter—despite knowing how hopeless and futile it was; the helicopter was traveling at tremendous speed and had reinforced glass like armor.

The helicopter was far off in the distance, having glided away from Little Havana.

"The fucks have got away!" Curry cried.

"Damn it!" Sam swore loudly.

"Our operation has been a failure," Curry remarked.

"The dealers will leave Miami," Dwane commented.

"We've caught most of the mobsters, but three Mexicans, three Cubans and two Americans have got away," Sam growled. "Two of them being the drug lords Jose Cortez and Juan Pazerra. The Americans upstairs must've seen us at the entrance and tipped off Pazerra via a mobile call. And that's how they gave us the slip. Very neat."

At that moment, Trogan, Rogers and Magee emerged from the rooftop door and approached Sam.

"Where are the eight remaining dealers?" Trogan wanted to know. "They got away?"

"You guessed right," Sam said. Then Chief Kavubu and Captain Olmera darted up from the steps onto the roof aiming their revolvers, before lowering them and replacing them into their suit jackets.

"We've captured twenty-five mobsters, but we've lost the two top drug lords and their bodyguards!" Kavubu rebuked Sam, Curry and Dwane.

"Don't be too hard on them, Chief," Olmera pleaded to his senior officer. "It wasn't their fault. The dealers were tipped off by two Americans who watched us coming. All eight men made a clean getaway, and that's why the helicopter was far away before Sam, Curry, Dwane and their back-up team could stop them."

"Okay, Olmera, I forgive them," Kavubu told the mustached Hispanic. The chief retreated to the door with Rogers and Magee, while the captain glanced coolly into Sam's face.

"Thanks, Captain," Sam told Olmera. "You got us off the hook."

"We've crushed the Juan Pazerra Cartel," Trogan boasted.

"But there are four other cartels," Curry said.

"And they're a threat to Timlook PD," Dwane informed Sam.

"Our friends Dave Bradley, James Mitchell and Nicole Lamenski need your help, Sam," Curry remarked.

"Me and some of my vice squad will take the FBI plane to Timlook Airport tomorrow morning," Sam agreed.

***

At Miami PD, Toby Ringwood was engaging in conversation with Chief Kavubu, Captain Olmera and District Attorney Michael Turillo in the DA's office. Michael Turillo was a black guy with a mustache and glasses, and his suit was dark gray.

"Dave and Nicole need me in Timlook with Dad's people, and I know I must go," Toby declared, his tone forceful.

"Why do they need you?" Turillo queried the young lawyer.

"To sort out the legal technicalities with the Courts of Justice in Chicago, Detroit and New York," Toby retorted. "It's a must."

"Why are they calling over a kid lawyer from the sunshine state?" Olmera inquired. "They can use their own lawyers."

"The Mck-Fee brothers are very dangerous men to cross," Kavubu snapped. "And even if you make it alive to New York, Cortez and Pazerra could have you assassinated as revenge against your father."

"I find it absurd that Sam would put his only son at risk," Turillo exclaimed.

"It was a joint decision between Nicole, myself and Toby," Sam insisted, appearing at the office door with his wife, Fiona.

"And Dave and Nicole agreed my involvement is critical in the legal negotiations," Toby said.

"What is your involvement exactly?" Olmera wanted to know.

"He means, why is it critical?" Kavubu inquired.

"To put it that way, yes," Olmera agreed.

"I'm a hot-shot lawyer with nine years' experience behind me, having passed the Bar exam at twenty-four," Toby explained. "But more to the point, when Dad's people crush the Jose Cortez Cartel, I will twist the arms of the New York lawyers to have Juan Pazerra, his two Cubans and two Americans flown on the next FBI plane back to Miami to stand trial. We can't convict them in New York."

"What's your objection to Pazerra's gang of five facing a judge and jury in the Big Apple?" Turillo asked.

"That's a question you need to ask Dad," Toby replied.

"The New York Police Department doesn't have enough evidence to prosecute Pazerra and his heavies," Sam informed the DA. "Due to the short period of time Pazerra's guys will have lived in the Big Apple, they won't have built up a criminal record long enough to warrant a severe prison sentence, but here in Florida, they have a record as long as the Pacific coast from San Diego to Seattle. The Miami police have more dirt on Pazerra, enough to hang him for good."

"And how does your wife feel about letting go of her only son?" Kavubu demanded.

"Toby is not my son," Fiona told the Kavubu. "He's my stepson. His real mother and sister died in a bomb explosion which was meant for Sam. This was before Sam met me and we got married. I care as much for Toby as Sam does. Both my husband and stepson lived through the grief and torment of losing the female side of their family, and so Sam knows what it means to lose people he loves. But he knows Toby must go."

"Toby's mind is made up," Sam agreed. "We're taking the next FBI plane to Timlook Airport, where we'll meet up with Dave Bradley's people. Not only Toby and me, but also Carrouso, Goldblum, Glen, Lopez and Clara. Six cops and a lawyer will be enough."

"You'd all better get a good night's sleep," Kavubu pointed out. "You'll need it. Tomorrow will be a long day."

"Goodbye and good luck," Olmera told Sam's people, his tone and manner cool.

Turillo grinned at Sam.

"You always get results, Sam." he praised the hard-boiled detective. "You said the New York Police Department has very little evidence to prosecute Pazerra's gang of five in their own jurisdiction, but here in Miami, we have tons of evidence that will hang those sons of a bitches for good. The biggest problem is finding them.

"Whatever happens, you and Toby must tell yourselves that Fiona loves and respects you both, and she knows that, through thick or thin, you'll both work as a team. We all have faith in you, Sam, Toby. And when the case goes against you, persevere. Never give up. Failure is not an option."

"Thanks for your vote of confidence, Mike," Sam said.

"We'll do our best, Turillo," Toby promised the mustached black lawyer. "The odds are ten to one we won't make it back alive, but we'll do our best."

"One question," Sam wanted to know. "You mind if I give Nicole one last call?"

"You mind telling me why?" Toby asked.

"To tell her the FBI plane will arrive at Timlook Airport tomorrow afternoon at three p.m. with us on board," Sam replied. "Nicole and Dave's Homicide Squad will meet us in the airport café, and they'll drive us in two squad vans to Timlook PD. We'll borrow their second squad van, spend the night at the department, and then Dave's people and the seven of us will take both vans and drive to Chicago."

"You have it all figured out," Toby said.

"I sure have."

Sam, Fiona and Toby left the DA's office, then Sam produced his mobile phone from his leather jacket.

***

New York's Bronx District was the city's roughest area and was dreaded for its gang warfare, muggings and murders, to name but some of the crimes. One street in particular was a no-man's land for the cops, and even heavily armed uniforms or riot police who dared enter it did so at their own peril. In a big stone building surrounded by a rundown car park was Jose Cortez's drug cartel, including Cortez himself, his two bodyguards and fifteen heavily armed Mexicans, two of them clean-shaven, five mustached and eight bearded.

Juan Pazerra, his two Cubans and two Americans joining the Cortez's cartel, increased its manpower to twenty-three, and as these rough-tough cutthroats stood on the building's flat, stone roof, a helicopter descended. The vehicle's speeding rotor slowed down before two black guys turned off the engine and opened the side doors.

The casually dressed mobsters were Matt and Ray Mck-Fee. The elder brother, Matt, was tall and muscular, his grin was evil, and his thick beard made his leering face even more menacing. The younger brother, Ray, was a thickly muscled brute who was cleanly shaven. His face was hard, cold and lacking emotion, showing he was an intimidating thug, ruthless, callous, and even more dangerous than his elder brother.

The Mck-Fees stepped down from the helicopter with three equally fearsome white men who were thugs. The first was dark and bearded with a smug, arrogant stare. The second guy was middle-aged with rough, brown hair, crooked teeth and glaring, aggressive eyes. The third man had long, whitish-blond hair, thin lips, sinister eyes and a cold, threatening voice like a Russian KGB officer. All five men approached the hardened criminals in the newly formed Cortez-Pazerra Cartel.

"We meet again, Jose," Matt snarled savagely. "You have quite an army here, and the car park and land surrounding this building are open areas, so the cops can have no chance of pulling one of their operations against you. Your private army of Mexicans would spot them a mile away and make mincemeat of those lawmen."

"And we see five men have joined your cartel," Ray said viciously.

"I am the leader of these five, Juan Pazerra," the Cuban called out. "These two Cubans and two Americans are my bodyguards, and we're from Miami. Sam Ringwood's vice squad crushed the rest of my mob, but your friend Cortez rescued us in the nick of time. Cortez and his two bodyguards told us we now owe him a debt of gratitude for our rescue, so we have joined his cartel and must pay off that debt by working with his Mexicans to have seven cops killed.

"I understand the four drug cartels, including yours in Chicago, have ended their gang war and have now united to massacre these cops, men and women from Timlook Homicide."

"Let me finish off," Cortez growled. "We also told Pazerra's guys how you, the Mck-Fees, are the brains behind this vendetta."

"It was our idea," Matt sneered. "Back in 2000, while our big brother James ran a drug cartel in Timlook, Ray and I ran a brothel in Chicago. James's cartel was infiltrated by a young policewoman called Melissa Morgan. Then, she and Detectives Dave Bradley and James Mitchell led a squad of cops in a shootout against our brother's mob in a car park, and the entire mob was massacred. James fought and nearly killed Bradley in one final brawl in the Metaxes Saloon, but Morgan rescued Bradley, aimed a piece at our brother and wasted him with five shots. The case was all over the Chicago news, and then the Chicago Vice Squad infiltrated our brothel before pulling a sting operation on us. At our trial, we were sentenced to fifteen years' detention in Illinois's maximum-security prison."

"But after nine years, the parole board did their work and we were released in March 2009," Ray said with a chuckle. "These three white men and a handful of black guys were also released, and together we formed the new Mck-Fee Cartel in Chicago, and we dreamt of how we would avenge the death of our brother, James Mck-Fee.

"We're sorry we couldn't fly down to Florida with your Mexicans to pick up Pazerra's men, but we had our hands tied cooperating with Sean Radeski's cartel in a close-range mob attack against Timlook PD. It was an attack designed to kill our brother's assassins and all the other cops who had been involved in his downfall and death."

"And then, due to our vast mob being too many men to fit with Radeski's gang on his plane, we withdrew from the operation," Matt Mck-Fee said. Radeski's people flew over from Detroit to Timlook and met up with eight men from your cartel. They used your truck to carry out the hit against Timlook PD, but, according to the news, the operation failed and eighteen of Radeski's thugs, plus your eight Mexicans and Americans, were slaughtered in two separate shootouts. We're sorry you lost those eight men.

"Radeski, Bergman, Pilski and four other guys flew back to Detroit in their private plane.

"Bradley, Mitchell, Manuchi and Morgan along with Lamenski, Reynolds and Ruiz massacred all twenty-six mobsters and survived the hit operation. Our personal vendetta against Bradley's people is now an obsession."

"I am forgiving," Cortez hissed. "But Radeski and his people are not. And they'll never accept the excuse that your mob would not fit onto his plane after losing eighteen of their people. Give Radeski a wide berth, meaning stay away from Detroit.

"They'll want Dave's blood if he and his homicide team ever set foot in Detroit. We also want these Timlook detectives out of the way, but if we attempt another hit now, the cops will see it coming. And now they'll be hunting us when they discover our involvement in the operation."

"Bradley's people are our problem, not yours," Matt growled. "You and Juan Pazerra worry about Sam Ringwood's people when they come to New York to bust you. Let my gang and Radeski's people deal with Dave Bradley's detectives."

"You mind filling me in on your plan?" Cortez demanded.

"All in good time," Matt replied.

"And where do we fit in?" Pazerra inquired.

"All we need to do is lie low and wait for Ringwood's people to venture inside New York," Cortez replied.

"You got it," Matt hissed. "But now, we must return to Chicago. "We'll see you again."

"Goodbye, guys," Ray said.

The Mck-Fees and their three mobsters opened the helicopter's side doors and leapt inside. Matt started the engine. The rotor spun round, and the helicopter ascended into the air, Matt and Ray glancing back to the mobsters on the roof below.

***

At Timlook Airport, while Dave, Jim and Dale were sitting at a café with Melissa, Reynolds and Bernardo, Nicole phoned Chief Tim Renko of Chicago PD to inform him that the Timlook and Miami detectives would arrive in Illinois the following afternoon to assist the Feds in hunting down the Mck-Fees. Then, she gave her Uncle Harry and Aunt Glenda Lamenski a call to tell them that both teams of detectives and a young lawyer were spending a few days in Chicago, and to ask if they were welcome to spend some nights at their place. Harry and Glenda agreed and, to Nicole's relief, felt no sense of danger with thirteen cops and a lawyer protecting them. The Lamenskis' place was a large rural house lying in the remote countryside ten miles east of Chicago. The detectives would keep the location strictly confidential, not even telling Chief Renko or the FBI. Once the mobile call was over, Nicole wandered through the airport terminal before rejoining Dave's detectives in the café.

"You made both calls, honey?" Dave asked.

"I have," Nicole replied. "Chief Renko and a squad of Feds will meet us at the department tomorrow afternoon and we'll go through the induction. And Uncle Harry and Aunt Glenda have agreed to have us to stay at their place on the condition we bring sleeping bags."

"Our sleeping bags are packed," Jim replied.

"But Sam's people," Nicole pointed out.

"They'll bring sleeping bags," Dale added. "How large is the house?"

"It's big enough," Nicole said.

"Sleeping bags are cool," Melissa said. "Not the height of luxury, but we'll manage."

"Sam Ringwood's people should arrive soon," Reynolds pointed out. "Why can't they fly us the rest of the journey to Chicago?"

"The FBI are not a ferrying service," Bernardo told him.

"And we'll need the two squad vans to drive through Chicago," Jim said.

"We've all eaten," Dave said.

"You had something to eat?" Jim addressed Nicole.

"I have," Nicole replied.

"What did you have?" he wanted to know.

"A big apple danish with fresh-squeezed orange juice. It was cool."

"Juice ain't freshly squeezed around here," Dave said. "It comes out of a packet."

"Yeah, yeah, okay," Nicole said with a chuckle. "It's the ultimate con."

"Temper, temper, lady," Dale bantered.

"Trust you to be sarcastic," Melissa joked, grinning shyly.

"Sarcasm is not your trait, Dale," Reynolds told the young detective.

"I keep it low profile, low key," Dale informed him. "And hey, we're over here guys!"

"Who are you calling?" Dave asked.

"It's Ringwood's guys!" Jim exclaimed with a laugh. "Why, you sons of bitches, welcome to Timlook. Come and join the club."

"Hi Jim, Dave, Nicole." Sam chuckled. "There's two Ringwoods here, me and Toby. Call me Sam."

"And call me Toby," the young lawyer said, his boyish face grinning.

"Not all of you know our fellow vice cops from Florida," Carrouso said evenly.

"You mind introducing yourselves?" Sam asked.

"Detective Martin Goldblum," the bearded hippy cop said.

"Detective Glen Hawke," the dark-haired, mustached cop said.

"I'm Detective Lopez Carreras," the medium-mustached Puerto Rican added, his youthful face smiling.

"And I'm Detective Clara Brown," the ordinary-looking blonde woman said.

"You all know Dave, Nicole and me," Jim said. He then introduced the others in turn. "We'll pick up our sleeping bags, spend the night at Timlook PD and leave in the morning."

"You have your sleeping bags?" Dave asked.

"They're strapped to our luggage," Carrouso replied.

"I never travel light," Toby informed him.

"You fancy having a bite to eat at this café?" Nicole inquired.

"We've already eaten," Sam said. "We brought sandwiches and fruit with us on the plane."

"I'm looking forward to meeting your Aunt Glenda and Uncle Harry," Toby enthused.

"Be my guest," Nicole said.

"Be our guests, honey," Dave added, smiling.

"Okay, be our guests," Nicole replied. She turned to the group. "We have two squad vans ready, but we'll drive both as the vice cops must relax."

Both teams walked through the airport terminal, exited the front entrance, and climbed into the vans. Dave and Jim punched their keys into the vehicles' ignitions and booted the accelerators.

***

It was at five p.m. the following day when Dave's detectives and Sam's vice cops arrived outside Chicago PD, vacated the vans and entered the building. They encountered Chief Timothy Renko, a squad of homicide detectives and a team of uniformed Feds from the FBI's Illinois Branch.

"Hi, guys." Renko greeted them. "I'm Chief Tim Renko, Head of Chicago PD."

"We're the men from Chicago Homicide," a Detective Inspector told them. "I'm Inspector Eddie Daniels."

"And we're from the FBI's Illinois Branch," a middle-aged captain informed Dave and Jim. "I'm Captain Nigel Lennon."

"Okay guys," Jim began. "Us five men and two women are from Timlook Homicide in Pennsylvania."

"Jim leads the team, not me," Dave told Renko.

"And we are vice cops from Miami," Sam announced, gesturing to his team. "This young man is a lawyer, and he's also my son, Toby."

"I'll handle the legal negotiations surrounding this case with the Chicago lawyers," Toby said.

"I'll run profiles on the Mck-Fee brothers, their fellow ex-cons and the rest of their drug ring before I brief you on any progress we've made on this case." Chief Renko concluded.

"Where are you sleeping the next few nights?" Inspector Daniels wanted to know.

"At Nicole's aunt and uncle's place," Dale said.

"The location is confidential," Nicole added.

"Tonight, we sleep here," Jim explained.

"We'll accommodate the fourteen of you," Renko agreed.

"Nicole must give her aunt a call," Dave said.

***

Both teams slept for ten hours before they woke up at eight a.m. the next morning. They climbed out of their sleeping bags and splashed warm water and soap over their faces in the washroom. Having had no time to eat breakfast in the kitchen area or even wash down a strong coffee, the casually dressed cops were summoned by Chief Renko into the main office.

Dave saw the glum, worried look on Renko's face.

"Bad news, guys," Renko addressed them.

"Bad news?" Dave said.

Renko nodded seriously.

"Come on, we're dying to know!" Jim insisted.

"Matt Mck-Fee made a mobile call from his van, so we couldn't trace the call," Renko began. "He told me a group of his mobsters murdered an informant and dumped his body either near the Christian church, the mosque or the synagogue. He hasn't told me which, but I reckon he's trying to split us into three groups so we're more vulnerable. So, exercise caution at all times.

"As you thirteen detectives ain't familiar with Chicago, three teams of uniforms will drive you in groups to these churches. Detectives Bradley, Mitchell and Manuchi, you'll investigate the synagogue. Backing you up will be Detectives

Reynolds and Ruiz. Detectives Ringwood, Carrouso, Goldblum and Hawke, you'll comb through the mosque. Detectives Lamenski and Morgan, along with Detectives Brown and Carreras, you'll come with me to the Christian church. We'll search everywhere. The informant's body is bound to turn up. Let's move."

***

Chief Renko, Nicole and Melissa searched the church's graveyard until they located the informant's corpse. The white male lay on top of a grave face-down with a gunshot wound to the back of his head, blood trickling through his hair and staining his torn denim jacket.

"Who found the body?" Renko wanted to know.

"I did," Melissa replied.

"We both found it," Nicole added.

"Trust you to take credit for something I did," Melissa objected, her feminine face frowning.

"Good work both of you," Renko praised them. "I'll join Carreras, Brown and the uniforms, who are waiting by the two squad cars, and bleep the other two teams that we've found the body. I'll also give CSI and Forensics a call. You two keep combing the graveyard in case a new piece of evidence turns up. Myself, James Mitchell's team and Sam Ringwood's team will be over here in ten minutes. I must go."

"Thanks, Chief," Nicole answered.

"We'll keep searching," Melissa replied.

Renko made his way through the graveyard and out of the church's entrance until he met up with Lopez, Clara and eight uniforms who were seated inside two squad cars, the first car flanking the church and the graveyard, the other positioned on the main street, blocking the street and cutting off traffic.

***

Waiting inside a large getaway van parked beside the pavement at the church were a mob of gunmen working for the Mck-Fees. Six thugs sat in the vehicle's main compartment and three long-haired guys were positioned in the front. They sneered and chuckled with evil hatred.

"They've fallen into our trap." The ringleader laughed. "The cops have split up into three small groups. Now we must execute the massacre and run. The Mck-Fee brothers will pay us handsomely for this."

They waited inside the van for another two or three seconds.

Part 2

All nine thugs in the van were terrifying rough-tough brutes whose hardened faces struck crippling fear into their victims.

The six in the back were three black men wearing Levis, T-shirts and leather jackets, two Mexicans in trendy suits and an Italian American dressed in a black suit with a grey raincoat over the top. The first black guy was stocky and powerfully muscled, with dense hair, a brutish face, a thick beard, and eyes that sharpened with the intimidating grin on his face. The second black man was slim and wiry, with a bald head and evil face, on which he wore glasses. The third had long, Rastafarian-style hair, a sneering smile, a thin beard, and he too was tall and well-muscled. The Italian American in the raincoat had medium-length, dark hair, a hard, serious face and cold eyes like a Mafia thug. The taller, slimmer Mexican was cleanly shaven, with a hard face and short rough hair, whereas the shorter, stockier guy had long, untidy hair, and a thick mustache on his chubby face.

The three leaders in the front wore jeans, casual shirts and loose denim jackets. The ringleader was a rugged, foul-tempered man with long, sweaty blond hair and an aggressive face. The second was stony-faced with medium-length, blond hair, evil eyes and a sneering grin. The third was taller but just as strongly muscled as the blond men, and he had a leering face and medium-length, black hair.

As the nine men clenched their high-velocity rifles, the ringleader addressed the dark-haired co-leader and growled his orders.

"Right, I want the Italian American and the Mexicans to climb into the front seats, and the Italian ready to bang on the ignition the moment the rest of us finish the job so we can scramble back into the van and make a clean getaway!" He turned to the blond co-leader. "You and the black guys will come with me to massacre the uniforms and then deal with Nicole Lamenski, Melissa Morgan, the Hispanic and the blonde bitch, and we'll take no prisoners.

"You will aim your rifle and cover us in case the operation turns messy. You got that?" He finished, addressing the dark-haired co-leader again.

"I got it."

"Right, you four, come with me!" the ringleader called.

The five mobsters jumped out of the van brandishing rifles as big as shotguns, and they advanced down the pavement. The long-haired black man reached for a small bomb inside the pocket of his leather jacket, ready to plant it underneath the first squad car in the street before the thugs turned their firepower on Chief Renko's uniforms in the second car positioned beside the church.

***

Lopez and Clara were talking to Chief Renko when they spotted the armed men advancing towards them.

"Hey, you bastards!" Lopez and Clara yelled, aiming their handguns.

The black man, caught off guard, threw the bomb towards the first squad car. It flew through the air and smashed through the windshield. The car exploded into a deadly fireball, killing all the cops inside.

Lopez and Clara reacted with violent, reckless courage. Clara fired three shots as Lopez fired another two, and all five bullets whizzed through the air and penetrated the chest and guts of the man who threw the device. He hurtled to the ground and died in the next five seconds.

The other four mobsters returned fire, and both Lopez and Clara were pumped and bloodied with four or five shots and crashed to the pavement, their mouths agape and their eyes big and devoid of life.

The driver of the second squad car punched his keys into the ignition, kicked the accelerator and raced the car towards the thugs. But the ringleader focused his rifle on the driver and pulled the trigger. The deafening gunshot echoed through the atmosphere. The bullet smashed the windshield and hit square into the driver's chest so that he fell backwards, then forwards onto the steering wheel. The squad car crashed hard into the back of another car in front of the thugs' getaway van, the almighty impact throwing the vehicle fifteen yards backwards so it stopped parallel to the entrance of the church graveyard.

The four thugs frantically raced towards Chief Renko's car, aimed their rifles at the windows from both sides and released all the firepower of their weaponry, killing all four uniforms and pumping bloody holes through Renko's head and body. The brutes showed no mercy or pity for the cops.

Nicole and Melissa heard the savage gunfire bellowing from the street as they stood over the informant's body in the graveyard.

"The others are in trouble!" Nicole cried.

"I'll radio for Jim and Sam's teams!" Melissa shouted. "I'll be with you in a minute! Hey, be careful!"

"Join me when you can!" Nicole sprinted across the graveyard and past the church towards the entrance.

For a few seconds, she froze. She saw Renko and the eight uniforms shot to death inside the two squad cars, the first car engulfed in flames and the second riddled with bullets and mutilated cops, with crimson-red blood gushing all over the seats and doors. She saw Lopez and Clara lying dead in a big pool of blood, and the four thugs now blazing their powerful rifles into Chief Renko's men. The blond leaders were firing from the pavement with their backs to Nicole, and the black thugs shot from the street, positioned between the burning squad car and Chief Renko's vehicle.

She was driven insane with rage, as if a fiery volcano had erupted inside her. Nicole darted towards the graveyard's entrance, training her handgun on the two blond men. She fired two ear-bursting shots into the stone-faced guy, and he fell backwards and hit the concrete before Nicole turned on the ringleader. The aggressive assassin spun round and aimed his rifle, but Nicole was close enough to dodge the weapon's thick metal barrel, thrust the rifle aside and throw a devastating kick into the man's crotch. Her hard boot caught his privates and the callous brute screamed with awful agony, doubling over around his legs and midriff. She seized his rifle and smashed the butt of the weapon into his rough face. It crunched into his temple and blackened his eye so that the ringleader blacked out and fell facedown onto the concrete.

The two black thugs were taken completely by surprise, just as their rifles had run out of ammunition. Nicole exploited the few seconds it took for them to reload, raised her handgun and blazed fiercely, felling the bald guy with two blasts before dropping the bearded man with another three rounds.

Her eyes shifted towards the bloodied corpses of Lopez and Clara, which was her fatal mistake, for she failed to spot the tall, dark-haired co-leader standing beside the getaway van. The big, muscular brute aimed his rifle towards her. She heard Melissa's voice yelling, "Nicole, look out!" and turned her head towards Melissa's voice, wasting precious seconds. The man squeezed the trigger and the lethal weapon exploded with a deadly gut-wrenching blast, before Nicole felt a large lead bullet penetrate between her breast and her left shoulder, ripping through the upper region of her heart and exiting her body through the shoulder blade. She fell, and her whole life raced through her mind as she crashed against and lay on the pavement, hanging on delicately to the ghostly spirit within her.

Melissa focused her handgun towards the dark-haired co-leader and fired four times, the volley of bullets slamming viciously into his chest, and he hurtled backwards and hit the side of the getaway van as he died.

Melissa lowered her handgun and screamed, "Nicole! Oh God!" but her concern undermined her vigilance and caution.

The blond ringleader, whom Nicole had knocked out cold, came round. He seized his rifle with both hands and spun the weapon towards Melissa. Aiming towards her midriff, he fired, but she had swiftly turned at an angle towards Nicole so the shot penetrated her arm just below the shoulder.

She screamed with the most hellish pain and skidded to the ground, the burning agony in her arm like a hot iron had gone in, as a river of blood streamed down her leather jacket.

The ringleader was off the ground and advanced towards the skinny brunette, his rifle aimed at her head.

"I'll send you to hell, you pig!" he snarled viciously.

But Melissa rolled onto her back, aimed the handgun upwards and pumped three savage blasts into his chest. The man let out a blood-chilling yell and hurtled to the concrete.

Melissa saw the two Mexicans and the Italian American coming out of the getaway van.

The men closed in on her, brandishing their rifles with murder in mind. Melissa's murder. They focused their deadly weaponry towards her as she lay on her side with her legs curled, leaning on her uninjured left arm.

"You remember James Mck-Fee who you murdered nine years ago," the tall, cleanly shaved Mexican said coldly. "His brothers are our bosses. And they want you dead."

Melissa was clenching her teeth and trying not to cry out with agony and fear, then saw Dave, Jim and Dale run past the getaway van and then halt and aim their handguns towards the mobsters' backs.

"Freeze, police!" Dale yelled, but Dave and Jim decided to open fire.

Jim fired three shots which killed the Italian American, while four shots from Dave's weapon dispatched the short, mustached Mexican. Jets of blood sprayed out of both sides of the thugs' bodies, and they crashed to the ground in the next four seconds.

The tall, clean-shaven Mexican spun round and blazed with his rifle, but Dave and Jim dived for cover, and then Dale fired. Four shots penetrated the Mexican's stomach and chest, and he fell in a spasm of death.

The savage shootout was over, but Dave was shocked and traumatized seeing Nicole lying splayed across the pavement.

"Nicole!" he shouted out with agonizing grief. "Nicole! Jesus Christ, no! Don't die on me, please!" He cradled his wife in his arms, begging her to live, his voice full of emotional torment.

"I'll call an ambulance!" Jim shouted frantically, and he raised his mobile phone to his face.

Dale hurried towards Melissa and held her diminutive body and injured right arm with his soft hands, the young woman sobbing from the agony and trauma of catching a bullet just below her shoulder.

"It's okay Melissa, you'll make it," he reassured her. "We'll get you to a hospital."

Melissa fainted against his chest, and he caressed her carefully, talking softly to her as she lay unconscious.

Dave was stroking Nicole's hair back from her face, talking to her comfortingly, as Reynolds, Bernardo and the four Miami cops arrived. Sam, Carrouso, Goldblum and Glen were horrified to see Lopez and Clara lying dead in a hideous river of blood, and Sam bashed Renko's car with violent anger.

"Damn it!" he yelled. "Jesus, God!"

"Chief Renko, Lopez and Clara never stood a chance," Reynolds snapped. "We're in for a war now. A war of impossible magnitude."

"Where's Jim, damn it?" Bernardo growled.

"I'm over here!" Jim shouted, as he ran back towards Dave and Nicole. "An ambulance for Nicole and Melissa will arrive any minute!"

"Check on Dale and Melissa," Dave advised Jim.

Jim hurried towards them as Dale cradled Melissa in his strong arms.

"She'll be okay," Dale said.

"She was lucky," Jim growled. "She was damned lucky."

"Not like Nicole here," Reynolds commented angrily, as the whining of the ambulances got closer and closer.

***

At Chicago's main hospital, Dave, Jim and Dale were briefing Inspector Eddie Daniels, Captain Nigel Lennon and Toby Ringwood on everything they knew about the shootout when the head surgeon and his medical team advanced down the corridor pushing a bed with Nicole lying totally unconscious on it.

"Hi, how did the operation go?" Dave wanted to know.

"We managed to mend the upper region of her heart," the head surgeon said. "The bullet hit her between the breast and the left shoulder and came out of her shoulder blade. It was lucky no arteries or blood vessels were hit. But her heartbeat is not very strong, and there's still a likelihood of death or brain damage. She will need to spend several nights here on a life-support machine for the best chance of survival."

"That's out of the question, Doctor," Jim informed him.

"Why is it out of the question?" Inspector Daniels objected.

"Without a life-support machine, she'll die!" Captain Lennon blurted.

"The danger of the Mck-Fees finding her is far greater," Dave said. "And then she'll die anyway. There have already been two hit operations against us. As soon as the Mck-Fees figure out Nicole and Melissa survived and are lying critical in a hospital, it will be their next target. And they'll have no hesitation killing innocent people. If we and hospital security get into a shootout with the mobsters, innocent people will be caught in the crossfire, including doctors, nurses and patients. We must drive back to Timlook and allow the FBI and the DEA to take over. We're way out of our depth."

"It's not only the Mck-Fee Cartel in Chicago we have to deal with," Jim told Daniels and Lennon. "Matt and Ray Mck-Fee run a network of cartels stretching from Chicago to the east coast. We know about the one in Chicago, the Radeski Cartel in Detroit, the Cortez-Pazerra Cartel in New York and a fourth in Boston. For all we know, there could be more."

Sam and Toby approached Dave, Jim and Dale.

"If we give up our vendetta against the Mck-Fees, there'll be a reprisal attack against my vice squad for that sting operation in Pazerra's cartel building," Sam began, "and if Pazerra's gang of five decide to take revenge against me, my family and my vice cops, they'll have Cortez's private army to back them up."

"And Nicole can't leave Chicago in her condition," Toby added. "The long journey to Timlook will kill her."

"Toby is right, Dave, Jim," the doctor agreed. "She's in no condition to travel."

"What do you suggest, Doctor?" Inspector Daniels asked.

"That she stays here, protected by security."

"Hospital Security will be no match for the Mck-Fees and their mob," Dave asserted. "These guys are extremely dangerous. They would heavily outnumber the cops and security guards and have more lethal firepower like rifles and possibly explosives. You not only have the security people's safety to consider, you have the lives of the patients and visitors at stake, plus your doctors and nurses.

"And Nicole doesn't have to travel back to Timlook with us. There's a place in the country where she can stay with her family and recover from her surgery, but for security reasons, the details are strictly confidential. If you have any records of her family's names, addresses and telephone numbers, you destroy them. You understand?"

"I understand," the doctor replied.

"So, our trip all the way to Chicago has been for nothing?" Sam asked.

"Not quite, Dad," Toby said. "If Nicole is recovering at her family's place, they will need protection."

"How do you mean, son?" Sam inquired.

"There's no guarantee the mob will not find out where Nicole is," Toby explained. "And if we return to Miami, we'll be sitting ducks for Pazerra's hitmen, or the whole Cortez-Pazerra gang. You, Carrouso, Goldblum and Glen can give Nicole and her family protection by hiding out at their place, and I'll stay with Nicole to observe any progress or recovery she might make, which I know is highly improbable. I've given the

Lamenskis a call and they're on their way to pick her up."

"Who will take over from Renko as Chief of Chicago PD?" Lennon asked.

"I'll take over," Daniels said.

"You'll continue combining Illinois's police resources to nail the mob?" Dave wanted to know.

"We will," Daniels reassured him. "It's best you people from Timlook make the journey back and continue your side of the fight in Pennsylvania. Sam's men and Toby will hide out at the Lamenskis' place and protect Nicole and her family."

"How is Melissa?" Dale inquired. "Has the bullet been removed from her shoulder?"

"It has," the doctor assured him. "But her arm is in a sling and will take two or three months to recover fully. The arm is in no fit state to fire a handgun if you run into these mob guys again, but she'll be discharged from the hospital in an hour."

"I told the Lamenskis they could hang about here for an hour or two before Nicole and Melissa were ready to leave," Toby explained. "They could have a coffee and their favorite apple pie and chocolate muffin while waiting."

"Thanks, Toby," Dave said.

"The Lamenskis have arrived," Jim remarked. "Hi, Harry, Glenda."

"Oh my God!" Glenda exclaimed. "Our poor niece!"

"Nicole!" Harry stammered. "How are you, young lady? Can you hear us?"

"She'll be unconscious for many days and may not survive," the doctor told them gently. "The bullet punctured the upper region of her heart. It's touch and go, so she needs plenty of tender loving care. And rest too, meaning she can't travel."

"Thank you, Doctor," Glenda replied.

"Shall we have a pot of coffee with a small apple pie and a chocolate muffin while we wait for Nicole to be ready? You fancy that, Glenda?" Harry suggested.

"It's the best way to pass the time," she agreed.

"I'll join you," Dave insisted. "And you can unburden yourselves to me about your grief. I'm upset too."

"We all are," Jim said.

Reynolds and Bernardo returned from the café with Carrouso, Goldblum and Glen.

"Can we return to the café, you guys?" Sam asked.

"We've just been," Glen said.

"We must eat," Sam told them. "You can just sit by."

Glenda and Harry kissed Nicole goodbye, and Toby and Jim offered Dave sympathy over the prospect of losing her, as they headed towards the café. But Dale remained with the doctor.

"You coming along?" Dave asked Dale.

"I must see Melissa," Dale decided.

"I'll take you through," the doctor offered.

"Thanks, Doctor," Dale said.

The doctor escorted the young Italian American to a different ward where they came to Melissa's door and knocked twice.

"Come in," she invited.

Dale entered Melissa's room and saw her lying in a warm bed, only wearing her pajama top so that her legs were completely naked.

"Hi there," he greeted his wife.

"Well, hi," she replied. "Am I glad to see you."

Dale leaned over and kissed her mouth.

"You took a lot of punishment," he said. "But Nicole is in a worse condition. The rifle bullet ruptured the upper region of her heart, but the surgeon has mended the damage and she's now about to be discharged. Her condition is critical."

"And I'm whining about this wound near my shoulder," she repented, feeling guilty. "You see my arm is in a sling, but at least I'm alive, so I must be thankful.

"When those three thugs aimed their rifles at me, you, Jim and Dave saved me. I owe you three my life."

"It was nothing," Dale said. "You would've done the same thing for us."

"Cops stick together through thick and thin," Melissa said. "What's on the menu for lunch?"

"We're having lunch at Glenda and Harry's place," Dale told her. "Glenda mentioned fish and veg stew with Idaho potatoes, followed by her favorite, walnut ice cream with maple syrup topped with chocolate."

"Oh yummy, yummy, yummy," Melissa enthused, her feminine face smiling. "Do they have hot chocolate?"

"I don't know, honey," Dale replied.

"Ughh," Melissa sighed, as she frowned. "I must be grateful for small mercies. I'm not the spoilt farm girl I was twenty years ago. I'm thirty-nine and you're thirty-seven, and the time has come for us to watch those calories. Otherwise, we'll lose our slim physiques and have heart attacks before we're fifty!"

"Old age hasn't worn us down yet," Dale said. "I'm as fit as a tennis pro and you're as skinny as a chicken, and you have nice legs. The nicest legs of any young woman your age." He winked at her playfully.

"Dale, don't," Melissa sighed. "You're embarrassing me, my love."

"Sorry, now is not the time to joke. Dave is emotionally crippled over what's happened to Nicole. Her life hangs in the balance. Chief Renko, his eight uniforms, and Lopez and Clara didn't make it. Sam's men are very upset. You're the luckiest cop of them all."

"That's a small comfort," Melissa said. "Nicole's number could be up, and Dave and Jim must be having a shit time. Give them my sympathy, my love."

"I will," Dale promised her. "And your arm will take two or three months to recover."

"No shit," Melissa replied. She was the worst cop in Timlook PD for using bad language.

Dale leaned towards her, and his lips met her plain lips, and she snuggled up under the blanket humming in her comfort. He caressed her forehead, stroking her hair back.

"Don't start to get comfortable, honey," he advised her. "We'll leave the hospital in half an hour. Now's the time to dress yourself and join me in the café."

"Okay, but please give me some privacy, honey, while I get changed."

"Your wish is my command," Dale said. "You know where the café is?"

"The nurses will tell me," Melissa said.

"I'll see you over there." He made his way to the door, left the room and walked back down the corridor.

***

Outside the hospital, the three thugs who had accompanied the Mck-Fee brothers on their helicopter trip to visit Cortez and Pazerra in New York were fitting a tracking device underneath Jim's squad van. The bearded man and the brown-haired mobster kept watch while the guy with long, white hair wedged the device near the brakes.

"You finished?" the bearded man demanded.

"I've finished," the white-haired guy replied. "The tracking device is linked to the Mck-Fees' mobile computer inside their van by radio signal. So, wherever these motherfucker cops drive, us and the rest of the mob will know where to follow them."

"Why don't we take advantage of our chance to kill the cops now?" the brown-haired man with crooked teeth said with a snarl.

"No," the white-haired mobster asserted. "There's more of them than the three of us. Our chance will come later when the rest of our gang back us up. Now let's go, before the cops see us."

The thugs wandered casually towards the Mck-Fees' van before Matt opened the back doors. Inside were Matt, Ray and four other black men sitting on two rows of seats on either side of the van.

"The tracking device is in place?" Matt asked.

"It is," the white-haired man replied.

Ray switched on the two computers.

"The first computer has a mapping system of Chicago," he began. "The second has a mapping system of the north-eastern United States, from Chicago to Philadelphia and New York. On both maps, the tracking device on Mitchell's squad van is indicated and will guide us to where the cops are heading. It will also show us where the Lamenskis live, and where Nicole is lying unconscious, if she's not already dead.

"The question is, if we're pursuing the cops all the way to Pennsylvania, how will we pull a hit operation against Nicole, her family and any cops protecting her?"

"We won't," Matt decided. "We leave that job to the rest of our Chicago cartel under John Lumumber and Paul Vaston. I'll contact Vaston on my mobile now and command him to await my orders.

"Our task is to pursue Dave Bradley's people, and at the very first opportunity, take them by surprise and massacre them. I won't rest until Dave, Jim and Melissa go down full of rifle shots."

"I can't wait," the white-haired man responded, his voice cold.

Matt fingered the digits on his mobile. There were four bleeps before John Lumumber, a fellow black mobster, answered. Matt told Lumumber his plan and then ordered Lumumber to put him on with the Frenchman, Vaston.

***

Night darkened the Lamenskis' country estate east of Chicago, and the detectives from Timlook and Miami sat around the dinner table, or on the armchairs and couch, enjoying platefuls of mutton curry with white rice.

Sam's vice cops and Toby unburdened themselves to the Lamenskis about their grief over the deaths of Lopez and Clara, and how, when the time came for them to return to Florida, an FBI plane would fly over to reclaim the bodies of all seven cops.

Dave's detectives shared with the Lamenskis their mutual grief over Nicole's condition and informed Harry and Glenda that they must leave in the morning and begin the long journey back to Timlook.

Nicole would recover in a single bed upstairs with Toby watching over her, with Sam, Carrouso, Goldblum and Glen protecting all three Lamenskis until the network of drug cartels was destroyed.

After eating apple pie with cherry ice cream, both teams of detectives climbed into their sleeping bags and succumbed to a well-needed sleep, their handguns positioned by their sides.

***

The following morning was bright and sunny, and Dave watched Nicole in the spare room as she lay half-dead in bed. He clenched his youthful face in his hands and groaned with grief. Many times he had come close to losing her, but now it seemed inevitable. A mixture of emotions grinded within his mind: grief, guilt and insane anger. Why hadn't he been there to assist Nicole when she needed him? Tears flowed from his eyes and he sobbed like a young boy. His body shook as he tried to come to terms with the probability of losing her.

"Nicole, I'm sorry," he groaned. "I'm so sorry. If you can hear me, please forgive me." He closed his hands in prayer. "May the Lord God give my wife extra strength to live. She is an honorable, brave woman. May the Lord also forgive my wretched soul for not being there when she needed me. Amen."

Toby came up behind him, and Dave jumped two inches from his chair.

"It's okay, it's only me," Toby said. "I know how you feel. I used to love her, and I'm trying to come to terms with the grief myself. You forgave us for the affair Nicole and I very nearly had nine years ago, during the Orlando Rivera Drug Cartel case in 2000."

"There was nothing to forgive, Toby," Dave said. "The feelings you had for Nicole were the normal, natural feelings of any young man. My wife is now forty-one, but she's still a young woman. Young, fit and strong. Maybe she'll come through this if God is merciful."

"God will be there for her if you're strong for her and really care," Toby told Dave. "Which I know you do."

"I'm now forty, but I still look and feel like a young man," Dave informed Toby. "I still have enough anger, strength and determination to carry on the fight. The fight for God, for peace and for truth, justice and liberty."

"We're both in the same boat," Toby added deeply. "I'm now thirty-three, and I've been a lawyer for nine years. But, I sometimes find practicing law is like walking through a minefield. The United States' policy of zero tolerance against crime really comes into question when you wonder why the Mck-Fees were released from a maximum-security prison after only nine years."

Both young men found it daunting that they would not stay young forever. Dave's mind flashed back to when he joined the Philadelphia police at the age of twenty-two, then Timlook Homicide at twenty-five. He was content with what he had achieved, as was the more youthful Toby.

The Tom Cruise lookalike kissed Nicole's face before Dave did the same, and then Harry and Glenda entered the room.

"Nicole was always a bright, intelligent woman," Glenda told them. "Brave, beautiful and determined. Being a cop was her life." She clenched her face and started sobbing uncontrollably.

Harry comforted her, and Dave got up from the chair to caress her shoulder gently.

"It's okay," Dave said.

"We're all here," Harry insisted. "Here for you."

Then, Sam and Glen entered the room.

"You okay, son?" Sam asked Toby.

"No, Dad, I'm not okay," Toby asserted. "But in case you're thinking of sending me back to Miami, forget it. My mind's made up. I'm staying here for Nicole."

"Toby, this is not the place for you," Sam insisted.

"Don't, Dad," Toby said. "I said I'm staying, and that's final."

"His mind's made up, Sam," Glen said. "He's a headstrong kid."

"And he's standing by you through all this," Dave told Sam. "That's what any son would want to do for his father. He also wants to be here for Nicole."

"I understand, Toby," Sam decided. "You can stay."

"Isn't it amazing that we don't appreciate someone we love, until we're about to lose them," Toby said. "Not that there was any real romantic love between me and Nicole."

"Not all love is romantic," Glen added, rubbing his mustache with deep thought.

"Thanks, Glen," Toby replied.

"I must return to Timlook," Dave announced. "Though I'm sure you will take good care of her, Toby."

"Nicole is safer here," Sam agreed ruggedly.

Jim appeared at the door. "We want to run you through a few important procedures," he told Sam. "Can all of you come downstairs? We're leaving in five minutes' time."

Everybody gathered in the large dining room, and Jim explained the procedures to the four Miami cops and Toby. Glenda and Harry listened vigilantly.

"We've disconnected the phone so that the drug barons have no way of finding your telephone number or address," Jim began. "The family's car and Sam's squad van are hidden behind those bushes, and we've taken the sign 'The Lamenskis' off your front door and hidden it. We advise all of you to keep the curtains closed, as if the estate is unoccupied, and to stay away from the windows at all times.

"If at any time you need supplies, ask Glenda and Harry to get them. They won't be so easily recognized by spies working for the Mck-Fee Cartel. The dealers can tell cops a mile off and word will eventually reach Matt Mck-Fee that Nicole is here, so, under no circumstances do you leave this house.

"Is that everything covered, Harry, Glenda, Sam, everybody?"

"That's everything, Jim," Sam concluded.

"That's everything," Reynolds agreed. "We all wish Nicole the best chance of life, but the five of us must head back to Timlook with Melissa. Jim, Bernardo and I have given our sympathy to the Lamenskis."

"I didn't get a chance," Dale said. He approached Toby and Dave. "To both of you," he began. "My sympathy is not enough, but I hope Nicole has the strength to pull through." He then turned to Toby. "Look after her and protect her. I know you will do that for Dave."

"Thanks, Dale, I appreciate that," Toby replied.

Then Sam, Carrouso, Goldblum and Glen each bade farewell to Dave and Jim.

"Good luck, all of you," Sam told the five Timlook cops.

"Thanks," Jim said. "We'll need it."

"Melissa is lying fast asleep in the squad van," Dale told Dave. "We'd better set off."

The Timlook cops departed through the front door, and then Sam set all the locks and burglar alarms on the door and the windows.

Dale, Reynolds and Bernardo opened the squad van's rear doors and leapt into the back, waking up Melissa who was lying down on the left row of seats. Dave and Jim climbed into the front seats and Jim started the engine.

It was a warm day outside.

"How's your arm, Melissa?" Dave called back, as Jim drove the van down the driveway and headed towards the highway.

"It's still hurting," Melissa replied.

"Any time you want to get things off your chest, tell us," Dave invited her. "I'm always happy to be a shoulder to cry on."

"I know you're here to protect me, Dave," Melissa said. "But I'll be okay."

Dave turned to Jim. "Where's our next destination?" he asked.

"Toledo," Jim said. "We have to drive east along the border between Indiana, Ohio and Michigan. We'll leave Lake Michigan behind us and go until we reach Toledo. We'll avoid Detroit, partly because it's way out of our way, and also because we don't want to run into Sean Radeski's guys."

"It makes sense," Reynolds called to the front.

"You bet it does," Bernardo agreed.

"Where will we stop off for lunch?" Dale addressed Jim.

"At South Bend in Indiana."

"That's where we stopped for a coffee break on our way to Chicago," Melissa added happily.

"Welcome to South Bend again!" Dale chimed in.

"Isn't Lake Michigan beautiful?" Dave said.

"It sure is!" Jim chuckled.

"I prefer the countryside of Indiana and Michigan to anywhere else," Dave said. "And our next destination, Ohio. The rolling prairies, the farmsteads, the fields of cereal crops and the woods scattered everywhere."

"The native Americans once owned the prairies," Jim began.

"Before the white men invaded their lands and forced them out," Dave continued.

"You're getting cynical, like me," Jim observed. "Even though I'm no ace on American history."

"I adapt to change, and America changes all the time, for worse and also for better," Dave said with a chuckle.

"History was written by the winners," Dale concluded.

"So, our next stop is South Bend," Melissa said. "South Bend, here we come."

***

At one of the saloon buildings outside South Bend, Jim, Reynolds and Bernardo were eating inside the bar area, while Dave, Dale and Melissa ate three baskets of chicken and French fries inside the van itself. Then Dave and Dale pulled two pieces of banoffee pie out of a white cake box.

"What did you get for me?" Melissa asked. "You know I don't eat banoffee pie. I like toffee, but bananas don't agree with me. Are two banoffee pies all you bought?"

"They only had banoffee pie for pudding." Dale smiled cheekily at his wife. "The saloon bar's special."

"Dale," Dave said. "Don't rile her. We also bought an apple pie."

"I was joking, my love," Dale said with a laugh.

"Dale, you son of a bitch!" Melissa joked.

"Hey, take it easy." Dale chuckled. "One apple pie coming right up."

"You do like apple pie, don't you?" Dave asked earnestly. "Only Dale decided to play a prank on you."

"Yes, I do like apple pie," Melissa replied. "And don't worry, I'm used to my husband's jokes."

Dale leaned over and whispered in Melissa's ear, "With your arm in a sling, do you want me to spoon-feed the tender apple pie into your sexy mouth?"

"If you leave the sexy part of it out," she replied quietly. "Yes, it would really help if you spoon-fed me. Or, better still, I'll take the spoon and use my left hand to feed myself." She stuck her tongue out at him cheekily.

"I hope the apple pie tastes cool," Dale remarked aloud.

"Thank you, guys," Melissa said. She leaned over and kissed Dale. "I know you and Dave would never forget about me." She put a giant spoonful of apple pie into her mouth. "Mmmm mmm, that is delicious."

"The banoffee pie tastes like heaven," Dale enthused.

"The hard banana chunks covered in toffee and cream really melt in your mouth," Dave commented, joking and smiling in a laid-back manner. "But they do better banoffee pie in Philadelphia."

"You think so?" Dale asked.

"I know so," Dave retorted. "Hey, what's that?" he exclaimed. "I hear movement outside our van!"

Dave's hand darted into his leather jacket and produced his handgun.

"You hear something?" Dale asked, also pulling out a weapon.

"I do," Dave whispered. "Outside."

Melissa's left hand reached inside her leather jacket for an automatic revolver, and she aimed it at the doors.

"You're scaring me, guys," she panicked.

"Relax, Melissa," Dave assured her. "You keep your handgun at the ready."

Dave and Dale focused their guns towards the back doors where they heard more footsteps.

"We'll check it out," Dale said.

"Are you ready, Mister, let's go!" Dave yelled.

Dave's hand pushed the handles down and they both pushed the doors open, jumped outside and realized their weapons were trained on Reynolds and Bernardo.

"Jesus Christ, you maniacs!" Reynolds shouted. "You scared the hell out of us."

"Point your guns away!" Bernardo called out.

"Hey, we're sorry guys!" Dale cried out. "We heard movement. You could've been anybody."

"We're sorry, Reynolds, Bernardo," Dave reassured them. "It was a false alarm."

"That's okay," Reynolds said.

"I haven't shaved for four or five days, my beard is quite a bit thicker," Bernardo added lightly.

"Mustaches suit us," Reynolds joked. "Beards do not."

Then Melissa's head popped out of the van.

"I see it's a false alarm," she said.

"Yeah," Dale replied.

At that moment, Jim came out of the saloon's doorway.

"What's going on here, guys?" Jim asked.

"Just a minor misunderstanding," Dave replied.

The journey to Toledo would be a long trip.

***

Inside the Mck-Fees' van, Matt and Ray and the other four guys watched the screen that showed the tracking device was leaving Chicago.

"The cops' destination is Toledo," Matt snarled.

"John Hazinski, Miles Carter and the De Marco brothers are hiding out in Toledo," Ray said. "With their mob based in Pittsburgh, they four will be no match for the six cops."

"No, but they own a helicopter," Matt said, sneering sadistically. "It is armed with missiles, which will blast a crater in the Chicago-Toledo highway. There will be a horrific pile-up involving dozens of cars and lots of casualties. The highway will be out of bounds for Dave Bradley's people. Mitchell's vehicle will have to come off the highway and head for Detroit, where Sean Radeski's mobsters will be waiting for them. Radeski's thugs are greater in number, better armed and more violent than the De Marcos.

"The cops will be caught between Radeski's people in Detroit and the nine of us pursuing from behind, each of the two mobs outnumbering the cops."

"How do you know the De Marcos will agree to blow up part of the highway and kill innocent people?" Ray asked.

"If they don't, I'll threaten to tell their arch enemies, the De Franco brothers in Chicago, where in Toledo and Pittsburgh they are based," Matt explained. "I'll give the De Marcos a call now."

Matt pressed the digits on his mobile phone and there were five bleeps before one of the brothers answered.

***

Flying from Toledo towards Chicago was a helicopter occupied by John Hazinski, Miles Carter and the two De Marco brothers.

Hazinski was a tall, overweight man with white hair, a thick military-style mustache and glasses, while Carter was a much younger man of thirty-eight, of medium height, muscular build and long, scruffy blond hair and a beard.

The De Marcos were big, stocky men in black suits with long dark hair and hard, brutal faces, like Mafia men. Both of them had been Mafia Godfathers in Chicago before the rival De Franco brothers' Mafia mob had exterminated their own. The De Marcos were now hiding out in Toledo and Pittsburgh with Hazinski, Carter and a private army of Mexicans and Americans.

"You heard what Matt Mck-Fee told us," the elder De Marco brother began. "We fail to blow a hole in the Chicago-Toledo highway and cut off the cops' escape route, the Mck-Fees will betray our hideouts to the De Francos, whose mob in Chicago is greater in number than the four of us after that brutal shootout where they massacred all our men and killed our family.

"But during the call, I told Matt there were strings attached to our agreement to cut off the cops' escape route. I said that if we blow up the highway, we want the Mck-Fees to arrange the massacre of the De Francos and their mob. The Mck-Fees have a large gang of thugs waiting behind in Chicago, led by John Lumumber and Paul Vaston.

"If Lumumber and Vaston are successful, I promised that if the six cops including Bradley, Mitchell and Morgan escape from Detroit, we'll lay a trap and kill them ourselves. The Mck-Fees were more than happy."

"So, after we blow up the highway, Lumumber and Vaston will pull that hit in Chicago and the De Francos' mob will be no more than bad memories," the younger brother said.

"Sounds real nice," Carter sneered.

"We're now within thirty miles of Chicago," Hazinski growled. "Time to load the rocket launchers."

"Missiles are in place," the elder De Marco remarked coldly. "And fire."

He pulled the helicopter's trigger mechanism and the missiles descended towards the highway with terrifying speed. They penetrated the highway with ferocious impact, and a series of vicious blasts exploded across the road, engulfing dozens of cars in enormous fireballs. Many more cars then crashed into the carnage of blazing vehicles. The crater left behind let off smoke from the twisted metal and smoldering tires, like a volcano.

"Now we'll return to Toledo to refuel, then fly back to Pittsburgh to rejoin our private army." The elder De Marco concluded.

The helicopter veered round and the De Marco brothers made another mobile call to the Mck-Fees.

***

Jim's squad van had left South Bend behind by five miles, and Dave fingered the vehicle's radio button looking for the Chicago News to hear any progress Homicide and the FBI might've made in hunting down the Mck-Fees. He found the station just as the news broadcaster reported the horrific pile-up ahead caused by missiles launched from a military helicopter with 'De Marco Brothers' painted on the sides.

"Oh my God!" Jim exclaimed. "It's a massacre." His jaw dropped with grief and horror.

Dave's eyes were sharp with indignation. "All those people murdered," he stammered.

"You heard what witnesses told the press at the scene?" Dale snapped, his voice full of emotion and sorrow for the victims.

"Yes, the name painted on the chopper's sides!" Dave replied. "So, the De Marcos are behind it!"

"The De Marcos survived a hit in Chicago a year ago, by a rival Mafia mob led by the De Franco brothers," Jim explained. "They had disappeared, but now they're another mob working for the Mck-Fees. Are we up against ex-Mafia guys as well as drug lords?"

"It looks like it," Reynolds said.

"Isn't there something else?" Bernardo began. "The Mck-Fees are behind the attack on the highway, and they involved the De Marco brothers—"

"In order to cut off our escape route to Toledo, then Cleveland!" Dale snapped.

"We must come off the highway and head for Detroit," Dave said fearfully. "Even though Sean Radeski's thugs are probably waiting for us there."

"We have no choice," Jim said. "The turn's just ahead of us." He took the exit towards Detroit. "Radeski's gang mean business, and they have more men and deadlier weapons than the six of us. We'd better be prepared for trouble, for I doubt we'll come out of this without a fight."

"We'll just have to find the next highway leading from Detroit to Toledo as quickly as we can," Dave added. "We never bargained for this, guys."

The vehicle continued its journey through Michigan, taking Dave's detectives closer and closer to danger.

***

Inside the Mck-Fees' van, nearing Detroit, Matt and Ray studied the second computer and watched the tracking device's movements.

"The cops are in Detroit," Matt snarled.

"And they're heading for Rockwood," Ray added, "to a hotel overlooking the Detroit River leading into Lake Erie."

"I'll give Sean Radeski's guys a call now," Matt said, producing a mobile phone from his leather jacket.

After four bleeps, Radeski picked up.

"Hi there, Sean Radeski answering your call."

"Hi, it's me, Matt Mck-Fee."

"You have a fucking nerve calling me, Matt," Radeski blurted. "After your men failed to back up my people in the operation against Timlook PD. I swore if I ever saw you again, the meeting would end with a bullet in your head. My mob would finish your mob for good."

"I had too many men to fit on your plane and then inside your truck," Matt growled.

"Excuses won't bring eighteen men and women back to life," Radeski said, his Polish accent threatening. "But I won't rest until Dave Bradley and James Mitchell are as dead as Abraham Lincoln. Why the call?"

"If you, Bergman and Pilski spare our lives and let bygones be bygones, my nine mobsters will help your thugs to massacre Dave Bradley's people," Matt promised. "Ten minutes ago, James Mitchell's squad van drove into Detroit and has stopped outside a hotel in Rockwood overlooking the Detroit River. Together, we will massively outnumber the six cops, and have powerful high-velocity rifles and grenades against their handguns."

"You say there are six of them," Radeski said. "What happened to the extra man in their group?"

"The extra woman, Nicole Lamenski, was critically injured in a shootout with my men, and the other woman, Melissa Morgan, sustained a gunshot wound to the arm," Matt replied. "Two Miami vice cops were killed, but another four Miami cops and a kid lawyer have taken Nicole into hiding at her family's place outside Chicago.

My back-up men in Chicago will soon pull a hit against the family home and kill Nicole, her family, the cops and the lawyer.

"I want your men to corner Dave Bradley's cops outside the hotel at Rockwood. They'll be up against five male detectives and a policewoman with a wounded arm and should finish them in minutes. We'll be there shortly."

"Okay, Mck-Fee," Radeski said. "We'll let bygones be bygones. My thugs will be over at Rockwood in ten minutes, but you'd better make damn sure you back us up this time."

The call was cut off, and Matt fingered the On/Off button of his mobile before placing it back in his jacket.

"Has Radeski agreed?" Ray asked.

"You'd better believe it," Matt sneered, a malicious grin reaching his beard, as their van entered Detroit.

***

The Lamenskis' country estate was surrounded by gardens, and Toby wandered through the north garden until he had reached the shore of Lake Michigan. His hand slipped into his brown leather jacket and pulled out his mobile phone, and he dialed the telephone number of Miami PD. With the phone to his face, five bleeps passed.

"Hi there, Miami Police Department in Florida, DA Michael Turillo taking your call," the mustached, black man answered. "Who's calling?"

"Mike, it's Toby Ringwood calling from Chicago," Toby explained. "Are Chief Kavubu or Captain Olmera around?"

"Hi, Toby, I'm afraid Kavubu and Olmera are having their lunch break, but I can pass on a message. What's happened to you and your father's vice cops over in Chicago? You want to fill me in?"

"It's bad news, Mike," Toby informed him. "There was a shootout outside the Christian church in Chicago. Chief Renko and eight uniforms were killed before Nicole, Melissa, Dave, Jim and Dale brought down all the mob guys. Detectives Lopez Carreras and Clara Brown also died."

"They died!" Turillo exclaimed. "That's awful! I'll tell the other cops and we'll inform their families. What became of Sam, Carrouso, Goldblum and Glen Hawke as well as yourself, young man? Are you all okay?"

"Me, my father and the other vice cops are okay," Toby told Turillo. "We're hiding out somewhere in the country protecting Nicole and her family. Nicole was critically injured, possibly fatally wounded, and she could die at any point. Nine years ago, there was chemistry between me and Nicole, and it's left me very upset. Melissa suffered a gunshot wound to her right arm, and now she, Dave, Jim and Dale along with Reynolds and Bernardo are running themselves back to Timlook.

"There's no chance of us carrying out police or courtroom cases in Chicago, Detroit, New York or Boston. Any legal battle is out of the question. And now we're in hiding, but for our own safety I can't tell you where."

"Okay, hang in there for as long as possible," Turillo insisted. "I'll pray for you and Dave that Nicole recovers. Even if the odds against her are a hundred to one, keep your fingers crossed.

"When you're ready to leave Chicago, give Miami PD another call. We'll send an FBI plane with Detectives Philo Magee, Enrique Rogers, Rogers' back-up, plus Jack Trogan, Jim Curry and Bruce Dwane along with four FBI Agents. They'll bring two coffins for Lopez and Clara. Sam's vice cops and Nicole will be flown to Timlook Airport. You will hand Nicole over to Dave and Jim, hopefully breathing, and then you, the vice cops and the Feds will continue the flight down to Miami. You got that?"

"I got it," Toby said. "I'll pass that message onto Dad. Good day, Mike." The call was ended.

***

The atmosphere at Miami PD was heavy with anticipation as Turillo replaced the phone. Behind him were Rogers and his team of four bearded hippy cops, Magee, Trogan, Dwane and Curry.

"You received a call?" Rogers asked.

"I received a mobile call from Chicago," Turillo explained. "It was from Toby Ringwood."

"What was it about, Mike?" Rogers wanted to know.

"There'll be no court cases against the four drug cartels in Chicago, Detroit, New York or Boston," Turillo informed the vice cops.

"No court cases!" Curry exclaimed. "What the hell happened, Mike?"

"There was a massacre committed by the Mck-Fee Cartel in Chicago," Turillo told them. "Chief Renko and eight uniforms were killed, and so were Detectives Carreras and Brown. Detectives Ringwood, Carrouso, Goldblum and Hawke are hiding out somewhere in Chicago with Toby Ringwood, protecting Detective Nicole Lamenski, who was critically injured in the attack, and her family. The other Timlook detectives are taking a long journey back to Pennsylvania to continue their fight against the drug cartels from Timlook."

"Oh my God, Lopez and Clara are dead!" Dwane exclaimed. "We must break the news to their families!"

"I'll phone Lopez's family," Curry decided.

"I'll call Clara's," Dwane said.

"As soon as their bodies are flown back to Miami, their families can make funeral arrangements," Curry said. "We need to break the tragic news to Chief Kavubu and Captain Olmera."

"They're coming into the main office now," Magee observed.

"What's this about us?" Kavubu wanted to know.

"It's about Lopez and Clara," Rogers told him. "They died in a shootout with drug dealers in Chicago."

"They died!" Kavubu exclaimed, his face in tortured shock.

"You all have my sympathy, including Sam Ringwood's men." Olmera comforted the Chief and everybody in Miami PD. "Their deaths are such a tragic waste." He turned and addressed Turillo. "Who broke the news?" he asked, his tone emotional.

"Toby Ringwood called from Chicago," Turillo replied, his voice frantic. "Toby and Sam's men are hiding out there somewhere. I feel really terrible for Toby, for Sam's vice cops and also for Nicole's husband, Dave.

"I told Toby to give us another call when they are ready to leave Chicago, so we can send an FBI plane over to collect them all.

"Are those Toby's instructions?" Chief Kavubu inquired.

"No, Chief, it was my idea," Turillo said.

"Okay, we'll wait for Toby's next call," Kavubu said.

"Now we let them lie low," Olmera explained, fingering his mustache.

"I'll take my lunch break," Turillo decided.

PART 3

At the Lamenskis' country estate, Toby walked through the kitchen door and greeted Harry, Glenda and Sam.

"Hi there," Toby said.

"Hi, Toby," Harry replied. "You took a long walk."

"Where have you been?" Glenda asked.

"Nobody is allowed to leave this building." Sam rebuked him.

"I was only in the garden near the lake's shore," Toby began. He told them all about the call with DA Turillo and the plan for when they were ready to depart Chicago.

"You've got it sorted out, Toby," Carrouso said with a chuckle.

"No, DA Michael Turillo has it sorted out." Goldblum laughed.

"They both sorted it out," Glen suggested.

"It was a joint decision," Sam concluded.

"How did our people at Miami PD respond to the tragic news?" Carrouso wanted to know.

"I don't know, I only got DA Turillo," Toby replied.

"How did he react?" Goldblum asked.

"He was shocked, horrified."

"Everybody must be," Sam assumed, stroking his mustache and stubble.

"I reckon so," Toby said.

"We checked on Nicole while you were out," Carrouso told him.

"And still no sign of recovery," Glen added.

"I regret turning her down when I had the chance," Toby said.

"We all know you loved her," Glenda added. "Nicole told us of your affection."

"It was traumatic enough when Glenda lost her sister, Nicole's mother," Harry said. "She died in a car accident when she was drunk behind the wheel. But now, we are about to lose our niece."

"There's nothing more terrible than outliving a younger member of your family," Glenda told Sam and Toby. "And Dave is facing the grief of losing his wife."

"Any one of us could've ended up a dead cop," Sam said, his voice bitter. "But why did it have to be Nicole?"

"She may still have a chance, Dad," Toby commented. "We just have to hope."

"Anyway, dinner is ready," Harry told his wife with a gentle smile.

"The table's already laid, Harry," Glenda said. "I'll serve."

***

They were gathered around the dinner table, having consumed chicken in orange and lemon, with rice and root vegetables.

"That was a cool dinner," Sam complimented Glenda.

"Agreed!" Toby praised her.

"What's next?" Carrouso asked.

"It's a surprise, Rico," Goldblum explained.

"But now, we're ready for the surprise." Glen coaxed Glenda.

"Are you ready?" Harry began.

"It's apple pandowdy," Glenda announced, her voice proud. "And it's cooling in the icebox."

"Well, I'm impressed, so let's all cheer Glenda," Sam said.

There was a chorus of cheers and clapping from everybody as Harry and Glenda smiled and rose from their chairs to collect the dish.

***

In the upstairs bedroom, Nicole was lying on the edge of death, and her spirit was trapped between her body and heaven. Her ghost was walking through mist, staring up into the afterlife when she saw the spirit of her mother.

"Mother!" Nicole exclaimed, frowning with surprise. "Where am I? What am I doing here?"

"You are a ghost, Nicole," her mother replied.

"A ghost!" Nicole frowned again, her teeth clenched. "What happened to me?"

"You were in a shootout outside a church," the mother explained. "You killed three evil men with guns, but a big, muscular man with dark hair fired towards you. The bullet went through your body and left through your shoulder blade, but your heart was in its path. You fell and hit the ground, and saw your whole life racing through your mind, but your spirit was trapped in your body."

"You mean my life is over?"

"That depends," her mother replied deeply.

"On what?" Nicole asked.

"On whether the Lord God is ready to take you into the afterlife," her mother told her. "The doctors mended your heart so it is still beating, but maybe it is not enough to save you from eternity. But the ghosts in the afterworld will welcome you when you're ready."

"And my husband, Dave?" Nicole pleaded, "And my friends? What has become of them?"

"They are on a journey," she said. "A journey in a van, which will take them through the cities and the prairies and over the mountains. Their destination is a big city, but they face a mountain of dangers. Groups of evil, wicked men are determined to destroy them.

"Your husband mourns your passing, but the peril that faces him and your friends may mean that they will join you in the afterlife. In eternity.

"But the afterlife is better, safer and cleaner than your previous life in the physical world. The good die young, but maybe the Lord God, whom your Quaker husband believes in, will make an exception for you. Only time will tell."

"Do you know if my friends will be okay?" Nicole asked. "Please, I must know."

"I'm not a fortune teller; I cannot predict the future," her mother remarked. "But as their journey is full of danger and violence, I doubt they will come out of the nightmare alive. It is an untenable and impossible situation they face, and the men of evil who want them dead are tightening their net."

"And I'm trapped in this world, powerless to do anything," Nicole sighed. "Well, I guess I must try and make the best of my predicament."

Her mother ascended into heaven, and Nicole sat down in the mist below, unsure what to do next.

I feel kind of lonely here, and I would give my left arm to have a friend to talk to, she thought.

* * *

On the pavement opposite the hotel in Rockwood, a truck skidded to an abrupt halt. Sean Radeski switched off the vehicle's ignition, then, along with Keith Bergman and Patrick Pilski, climbed out of the truck and headed towards the rear. Radeski opened the rear doors and eight men leapt out. The three ringleaders and their back-up pulled eleven rifles out of the main compartment, then shut the doors and made their way behind two limousines parked across the street from the hotel's doorway.

Five of the back-up mobsters were casually dressed and the other three wore suits. Two of the casual men had medium-length, brown hair and boyish faces, while a third was over forty with a muscular build, short dark hair, a leering face and screwed-up eyes, and a fourth was in his early thirties with short, fair hair and an aggressive face. The fifth casually dressed guy was the same well-built Pole with long brown hair and a bald patch over his head who had met up with Radeski, Bergman and Pilski on the airstrip outside Timlook.

Walking behind these five rough-looking thugs and the three ringleaders were the three ex-marines in suits, including the grey-haired Nick Sommers, the blond, mustached guy wearing sunglasses and the black man with a mean face. All these brutes fingered the triggers of their rifles as they aimed towards the hotel's front door.

***

Having all swirled down a few drinks in the bar, Dave, Jim and Dale emerged from the hotel ahead of Melissa, Reynolds and Bernardo, and immediately spotted the armed men aiming their rifles towards the entrance.

"Everybody, get down!" Dave yelled.

All six detectives dived towards the concrete as the men opened fire with a barrage of ferocious gunshots which pumped holes into the woodwork. Within the next few seconds, Dave's people had crawled to the squad van and reached for their handguns.

"Reynolds, Bernardo, Melissa!" Dave cried. "Get into the front and drive to the gas station outside Rockwood! We'll join you there in half an hour's time!"

"Okay, let's go!" Reynolds shouted.

Melissa pulled open the driver's door and leapt over the driver's seat into the main compartment. Reynolds and Bernardo crawled across, shielded by but the van's bullet-proof windows and windshield.

Reynolds banged the key into the ignition, then kicked the accelerator and the van sped along the street heading south towards the gas station.

Dave, Jim and Dale made their way behind a blue Volvo before they retaliated with deadly violence. Dave fired four shots which felled the dark-haired man with a leering face and screwed-up eyes, while Jim and Dale pumped ten blasts into the two young men. All three thugs hurtled to the pavement, their limbs splayed in an undignified manner, their chests smeared with blood.

The other mobsters continued blazing with intense ferocity, and the detectives knew they would stand no chance out in the open and armed only with handguns, outnumbered and outgunned.

"Get inside the hotel!" Jim ordered.

The detectives raced through the hotel door and hurried past reception, back to the corridor running parallel to the bar area.

"We'll separate to confuse them," Dale said. "I'll go upstairs and find a laundry room!"

"What do you mean a laundry room?" Dave snapped.

"Just trust me!" Dale insisted.

He turned and charged up two flights of stairs, while Dave and Jim sprinted towards a door leading downstairs into the basement.

***

The mobsters were inside the hotel only a few seconds behind and saw the detectives splitting up.

Radeski ordered the fair-haired guy and Nick Sommers's ex-marines to head upstairs after Dale, and for the four Poles to pursue Dave and Jim into the basement. They all sprinted off as they were told.

The Poles in the basement encountered many rows of shelves across a massive cellar. They spotted scuff marks on the floor from Dave and Jim's shoes leading down an aisle, and they hurried to follow them before the trail split into two directions.

"Bergman and I will turn left while you two go right," Radeski snarled.

Radeski and Bergman headed left down an adjacent aisle, but the trail ran cold. The balding man and Pilski went right and searched behind a crate of beers.

***

Dave and Jim were lying in wait on top of the shelves in each direction. Dave jumped down, pointed his handgun towards the balding man and, with a single blast, sent a round through his head, killing him instantly. Pilski spun round and aimed his rifle, but Dave fired twice, the hot lead penetrating Pilski's head and throwing him backwards against the crate of beers. As Radeski and Bergman aimed their rifles in Dave's direction, the young detective took cover behind the shelves. Five exploding gunshots echoed through the basement, sending hot bullets slamming into another crate. At that moment, Jim leapt down from the left row of shelves, aimed his handgun, and two shots to the back of Bergman's head finished him.

"You scum, Mitchell!" Radeski growled in fury.

The Pole swung round sharply and charged at Jim, focusing his rifle. Jim instinctively deflected the barrel away from his head and the gun exploded with a terrifying blast, the recoil knocking Radeski backwards.

Radeski grabbed one of the shelves and pulled himself back onto his feet. Jim seized him and punched the Pole square in the stomach, then landed another fearsome blow into his face, so that his mouth started bleeding. Jim grabbed Radeski's arm, and banged his elbow against a shelf, trying to force the rough-tough killer to release the rifle, but Radeski swung his arm round to break Jim's grip and threw a savage punch into Jim's stomach and two more into his face. The blows bloodied Jim's nose and mouth, blinded him with tears and sent him hurtling to the floor. Spinning his rifle back round with deadly speed, Radeski aimed at Jim, his eyes sharp with hatred.

But Dave had crept up behind Radeski, and with his handgun aimed towards Radeski's head, squeezed the weapon's trigger twice. His head spewing blood, Radeski awkwardly plummeted to the floor.

Dave hurried towards Jim, who was coughing from the blow to his stomach, and his nose and mouth were streaming blood.

"Are you okay, Jim?" Dave fired his words out.

"No way, damn it!" Jim growled. "But thanks, Dave, I owe you one!" Jim cleared the blood from his beard.

"We'd better find Dale," Dave said. "I don't know what he's up to."

***

Dale was on the second floor of the hotel when he found the laundry room. The door was locked, but with all his weight and strength, he bashed it open and hurried in.

His thinking behind separating from Dave and Jim was to weaken the mobsters' numerical strength by splitting them up, evening the odds in a gun battle. And he chose the laundry because there would be a laundry chute leading down to the basement. If the mobsters were too many to fight off, he would dive down the chute and rejoin Dave and Jim.

Dale located the chute, and then hid behind one of the shelves nearest to it, knowing he was outnumbered four to one. The fair-haired thug and the three ex-marines arrived at the laundry room, and Nick Sommers was the first to charge in. Dale's handgun exploded with four savage blasts which bloodied the old man's chest and killed him outright. The fair-haired mobster, the blond, mustached brute and the black thug fired towards Dale with terrible ferocity and then retreated into the hallway, but Dale was not about to waste rounds by fruitlessly firing back.

The two marines produced four grenades from their jackets and then slung them across the laundry. One rolled casually towards Dale's feet. Dale panicked and screamed with fury as he ran for the laundry chute. He leapt in and fell head and arms first down towards the basement. The whole laundry erupted with four fiery explosions, which shattered the foundations of the room and sent a fierce spurt of fire blazing down the chute, narrowly missing Dale as he fell. He landed hands first onto a pile of towels and then rolled head over heels out of the chute and into the basement.

"He survived!" the black man shouted angrily to the blond guy and the fair-haired thug. "He's in the basement where Bradley and Mitchell are hiding! Damn it guys, we must move!"

Dale heard this, and he raced along the aisle, focusing his handgun, until he met up again with Dave and Jim.

"That was good thinking, Dale," Jim complimented the young man. "You cut their strength in half."

"But they know I fell into the basement," Dale said. "There's three of them left, and they're coming down here now."

"We're ready for them," Dave said. "We'll hide behind the shelves nearest the stairs."

The cops took their positions, and it was only a short minute before the mobsters ran through the basement door and down the stairs. Dale pumped three exploding shots into the mustached marine, killing him instantly. The other two thugs blazed with their rifles a split second after Dale retreated behind the shelves again. Then Dave and Jim emerged, Jim dispatching the black marine with three roaring shots, while Dave dropped the fair-haired thug with four.

All three thugs were sprawled across the basement floor, rivers of blood running from their chest wounds, their eyes empty with death. The detectives replaced their weaponry inside their leather jackets.

"These were Sean Radeski's men," Dave said.

"Hired by Matt Mck-Fee," Jim added.

"We've destroyed what was left of Radeski's cartel," Dave explained. "But I have a hunch the Mck-Fees' mob have pursued us all the way from Chicago and will storm into the hotel any moment. They could be waiting outside the front door right now, ready to back up Radeski's guys or cut off our escape route.

"We'll leave through the back door, escape through the gardens overlooking Lake Erie and then make our way through Rockwood to join our friends."

"We'll follow," Jim said.

"We must find Melissa, Reynolds and Bernardo at the gas station," Dale added. "Let's move."

The cops raced up the stairs and out of the basement and heard the Mck-Fee brothers talking to their thugs outside the hotel's front door.

"Follow me to the back door," Dave whispered.

***

They reached the gas station within the next half hour, and Reynolds and Bernardo greeted them.

"You took your time," Bernardo said. "We must move."

"It's five p.m. and evening is approaching," Reynolds pointed out.

"We must get far away from Detroit," Dave suggested. "Then drive through Toledo and keep driving until we reach Cleveland. When we get there, we can have a bite to eat at a saloon outside the city."

The detectives hurried into the squad van, Reynolds and Bernardo jumping into the front seats again, with Reynolds driving, and Dave, Jim and Dale rejoining Melissa in the van's main compartment.

***

The next part of the journey took the better part of five hours. Reynolds drove the van round Toledo before continuing along Ohio's highway overlooking Lake Erie. He bypassed Cleveland city center and then took the highway leading to Akron. On the way, he located a saloon building with a massive car park. He careered through the entrance and between two rows of cars, and then parked two spaces in, parallel to a truck a few spaces away. The van was well hidden from the entrance in case the Mck-Fees drove in.

Dave glanced towards his watch. It was ten p.m.

"Are you guys hungry?" Reynolds wanted to know.

"I am," Bernardo replied, his stomach growling.

"I could eat a buffalo," Reynolds said.

"I'm dying for a meal," Jim commented. "I'm getting much thinner."

"We all are," Dave remarked.

"I'd rather stay in the van keeping watch," Dale told Dave.

"I'm tired," Melissa groaned. "Just bring me a box of pizza for when I wake up."

"I'll stay with you," Dale promised his wife. "I'll share the pizza with you."

"Yes, we're all hungry," Dave told Reynolds.

"All except Melissa," Jim added. "But I'm sure the bar has pizza she can have later."

"Most saloons serve pizza," Dave said. "Ready to go, guys?"

The detectives left the van, leaving Dale and Melissa inside, and made their way through the saloon's doorway into the bar area. Melissa succumbed to a deep sleep.

Dale waited until he was sure Melissa was fast asleep and then vacated the vehicle for a taste of the fresh evening air. He had only been outside for a few minutes when he spotted a large van speeding through the entrance of the car park. It parked in a space near the entrance, with its rear doors facing the saloon building, before three white men climbed out of the front.

Dale hid behind the squad van's left rear door and glanced with horror towards the Mck-Fee brothers and four other black guys jumping out from the vehicle's main compartment brandishing rifles.

How come the Mck-Fees always know where we're heading and which highways to pursue us down? This question grinded at Dale, but what was certain was that the detectives would never shake the Mck-Fees off their trail.

Dale considered his options. Dave, Jim, Reynolds and Bernardo were sitting in the saloon's bar area; it would be four cops against nine better-armed mobsters. If it came to a shootout in the bar, the detectives would be extremely vulnerable, not to mention the fact innocent people would be caught in the crossfire. Joining Dave's team would only increase their manpower by one, and he could not leave Melissa alone, fast asleep, her right arm still incapacitated. She would be no match for nine mobsters. His mind was made up; he must get Melissa to a safe hiding place.

There were five spaces between the squad van and the truck, each one occupied by a car, measuring a total distance of twenty-one yards. Dale and Melissa would need to cover this distance and hide underneath the truck before the Mck-Fees and their thugs reached their van.

Dale climbed back into the squad van and quietly made his way towards Melissa. He shook her awake, whispering to her at the same time, and as she awoke, he pressed his hand tightly over her mouth to prevent her crying out with fear. As his hand covered her mouth, Melissa's face frowned up at Dale and her eyes flickered slightly.

"Don't make a sound," he whispered. "You must get up now and come with me. There is danger nearby." He removed his hand from her mouth.

"Dale, what's wrong?" she asked nervously.

"Mck-Fee's men are in the car park," Dale replied. "They know we're here. Don't ask me how, they just know. And they'll be here in a matter of seconds. Come with me now."

Melissa got up off the right row of seats, and both she and Dale climbed quietly outside. Her right arm was still painful inside its sling, and she gritted her teeth as sharp agony shot through the injured limb. They stooped as they walked along the van's right side, then made their way behind the five cars towards the truck, Dale easing Melissa along.

"It's okay now, you're doing fine," he said. "Head for that truck over there."

They reached the truck and Dale helped his wife onto the ground and ushered her underneath the trailer. Melissa's face strained from the pain in her arm, but she fought not to utter a sound. Dale lowered himself beside her, making it in the nick of time. They saw the nine thugs approaching the squad van and glancing through the open doors.

"They must be somewhere," they heard Matt insist.

The thugs scrambled inside the van and glanced underneath.

"They're not here." Matt addressed Ray. "They knew we were coming. They might be in the restaurant."

While Dale and Melissa were watching Matt Mck-Fee's men, the worst burning agony tortured Melissa's arm and she groaned like a child. She pressed her left hand tightly over her mouth to stifle her voice. Dale stroked her hair to reassure her through the intense pain.

Dale heard Matt and Ray order the other four black men to stay by the van while they and the three white men would check each car and the truck to find out where the groans were coming from.

All five thugs made their way behind each car, looking inside suspiciously, but found them empty. Then they came to the truck, clutching their rifles. Dale and Melissa were obscured in the blackness underneath the truck, but a single sound would give away their position.

Melissa tightened her bony hand over her mouth, her sharp eyes flickering due to the burning agony in her arm. Dale gently caressed her head.

"I swear I heard groaning," Matt whispered to his thugs.

"There's nobody here," Ray said. "We're wasting time. The cops are inside the saloon bar."

The five men hurried to rejoin the four black guys positioned by Jim's vehicle, then the armed mob approached the saloon's doorway and entered the bar.

The pain in Melissa's arm eased itself but her face appeared tortured.

"Dale, I'm scared," she wept pitifully.

"I'm scared too," he replied. "But I'm going to go shoot the tires on the Mck-Fees' van. Stay here until I come back."

"Please, be careful," she begged him.

"I'll be careful," was his thoughtful reply. He dragged himself between the truck's tires, ascended to his feet and ambled towards the Mck-Fees' van, pulling out his handgun. He would puncture the van's tires with four quiet shots, one to each tire. He would muffle each shot by pressing the barrel of the weapon firmly against the hard rubber.

He pressed the trigger, and a gunshot penetrated the first tire.

***

Dave, Jim, Reynolds and Bernardo were sitting at a large table when they and Mck-Fees' men spotted each other. Matt and Ray ordered nine beers, and then approached the table where the cops were sitting, backed up by the three white men. The other four sat around the bar. The detectives eased their hands towards the guns inside their leather jackets, pulled out the fearsome weaponry and aimed the pieces underneath the table.

"Well, well, look who we have here," Jim boasted to Dave. "We have company."

"Just play it cool," Dave advised the others.

The five mobsters descended into some seats on the other side of the table.

"We don't recall inviting you to our table," Reynolds snapped, his face screwed up with anger. "You have a hell of a nerve crossing our path."

"Play it cool, John," Dave insisted. "We're not out to start a shootout in a respectable saloon bar."

"That's very wise, Bradley," Matt remarked, a sly grin across his face. "Us mobsters may be dirty in our methods, but we are clearly men of class. High-class businessmen."

"You mean high-class sewer rats," Jim said.

The white-haired mobster and the brown-haired thug, taking offence to Jim's remark, scrambled up from their seats and took aim at the cops with their rifles.

Matt diffused the situation, "It's okay men, we're big enough to take insults," he sneered. "Sit down. We must negotiate with them."

"You're wasting your time, señor," Bernardo growled. "We don't negotiate with scumbags. Especially when they try to burn us out."

"My wife Nicole is hanging onto life by a thread because you tried to kill her and Melissa," Dave snapped. "Two other cops died, Lopez and Clara. So kindly refrain from pretending you have class and get to the point."

"We don't have all day," Jim added.

"I'll get to the point," Matt said. "We've decided to spare your lives if you tell us where Melissa is. We're really after her, not you or Dale."

"Sorry pal, we don't sell out our own people," Jim growled in a hostile manner. "So, if you want to kill us, we're dying for a damn good fight."

"And don't forget, we're the four best cops in the business," Reynolds boasted, as they all readied their handguns underneath the table and fingered the weapons' triggers.

"Wait guys, there's no need for any violence," Dave steadied his men. "There's innocent people in here." He turned towards Matt. "You guys want Melissa dead for the way she killed your brother, James?"

"You guess right," Matt hissed. "Remember August 2000? Nine years ago? She killed our big brother, and then we went to jail for nine frigging years."

"It was a shootout in a saloon," Dave snapped. "Your brother was going to kill me, and Melissa was only protecting me. She saved my life."

"But James is dead because of her," Matt said. "And we won't rest until she faces the ultimate justice for her crime."

"You know nothing about justice, señor," Bernardo said. "Drug dealers like you have contempt for justice and contempt for humanity. We won't sell out Melissa because she is protected by our code of loyalty. She killed your brother in self-defense."

"So go back to your rathole, pal," Jim growled sullenly. "You'll get no cooperation from us."

"Do you understand?" Dave snapped.

"Very well, Mitchell, Bradley." Matt laughed, his sneer evil and malicious. "I'll explain your dilemma. Nobody can hide from the Mck-Fee Cartel. We find people. We know where Dale Manuchi's former house is in Pittsburgh, and where Melissa Morgan's place is, the farm in the country. As for you, Dave. We know where the Quaker hamlet is outside Philadelphia, where your family lives, and we know where Nicole, her Aunt Glenda and Uncle Harry are in that country estate ten miles east of Chicago. We know because we've searched the telephone directories covering Illinois and Pennsylvania. If you don't tell us where Dale and Melissa are hiding, you, your wife and your Quaker family will spend the rest of your lives running away from us, looking over your shoulders. We can also find out where Jim's ex-wife lives—"

"Now you're getting nasty, sucker," Jim snarled, his eyes sharp.

"Let me finish, Mitchell," Matt demanded. "The net will close in on you fast. The New England Net, as we call it. I have men in Chicago who are ready to attack Nicole's house and waste her, her uncle and aunt, and those four Miami cops left alive. I will soon send men to the Quaker hamlet to kill the Bradleys. And eventually, we'll find Dale and Melissa, and kill them too. You can't hide from us, Dave, Jim. Nobody can. If you hide, we'll find you.

"And now, our drinks are at the bar, so we'll rejoin our men and guzzle down our beers. Good day, Bradley."

"A great speech, motherfucker," Reynolds remarked, his voice hostile.

"Your threats don't intimidate us, you bastards," Bernardo growled. "You come to within twenty yards of us and we'll kill you."

"It's the last mistake you'll ever make," Dave cried out.

At that moment, the waiter delivered two cardboard boxes of pizza onto the detectives' table. All four of them produced their wallets and contributed a few dollar notes for the pizzas and the drinks they had swirled down.

"Thanks, waiter, you can keep the change," Dave told him politely.

"Time's running out," Jim said. "We'd better leave."

"Then let's go," Dave told the others.

They saw the Mck-Fees and their mob sitting at the bar with their backs to them, sipping beer from their glasses and totally unaware the detectives were about to give them the slip.

The detectives left the table and made their way to the exit. They returned to the squad van to find the rear doors open.

"Where are Dale and Melissa?" Jim asked.

"We're over here," Dale replied. He was guiding Melissa behind the five cars away from the truck and towards the other detectives.

"The Mck-Fees tried to pull a deal with us," Dave said to Jim. "They don't want us dead, they want Melissa."

"Why Melissa and not us?" Dale asked frantically.

"I killed their brother," Melissa pointed out.

"We'd better run, before they come out of the saloon," Jim said. "We're lucky they didn't try to kill us."

"Too many witnesses," Reynolds explained.

"Witnesses who'd testify and send all nine of them to the joint," Bernardo remarked.

"Let's get out of here," Dave said, his voice frantic. "We'll save the pizza until later."

"Hop in, guys," Jim ordered. "I'll drive."

Dave and Jim jumped into the front seats while the other detectives leapt into the main compartment and slammed the doors shut. Jim banged his keys into the ignition, thrust his foot onto the accelerator and sped round behind the five cars and the truck. The van raced back through the car park and veered out of the exit onto the highway. The vehicle sped at fifty miles per hour towards Akron on the Ohio-Pennsylvania border.

"If we don't stop the Mck-Fees, they'll target my family's place outside Philadelphia, Jim's ex-wife's place in New York, the Lamenskis' country estate and Dale's old house in Pittsburgh," Dave explained fearfully. "They know where Melissa's farmstead is in the countryside outside Timlook."

"They know Nicole's uncle and aunt are called Harry and Glenda," Jim added, terrified. "That they are being protected by the four Miami cops and a young lawyer, and that the place is a big country estate ten miles east of Chicago."

"This is serious," Dale cried.

"How did they find out all this?" Melissa asked.

"Using telephone directories," Jim growled. "They searched under our surnames, and there ain't that many people in Illinois and Pennsylvania called Lamenski, Manuchi, Morgan or Mitchell. Or even Bradley, which is more common."

"There's more to it," Dave informed Jim. "The Mck-Fees must've had us followed when we drove Nicole from the hospital to the estate. And Sam's men, Toby, Harry and Glenda were there too."

"If they'd had us followed, we would've hatched onto the pursuit long before we reached the estate," Jim told Dave. "And nine of them wouldn't have been stupid enough to take on four Miami cops and the six of us altogether, we'd be ten detectives against nine thugs. And the country estate is easy to defend with many hiding places from which to take the thugs by surprise."

"Another thing's bugging me," Dale remarked, his manner inquisitive.

"You'd better tell us," Melissa said.

"How did they know we'd take this route? The highway from Cleveland to Akron? And how come they knew we'd stopped off at that particular saloon on the way? And once we had parked our van, we took special care to make sure it was well-hidden and yet, the Mck-Fees and their thugs found it within seconds."

"Dale and I had to hide underneath the truck, which was positioned five cars from the van," Melissa told Dave. "My arm hurt badly, I whined and groaned because the pain was too much, and the Mck-Fees nearly found us. We're lucky to be alive."

"Even more to the point," Dave began again. "How did Sean Radeski's thugs in Detroit discover where we'd stopped off for drinks at that hotel in Rockwood? Soon after we dispatched Radeski's guys, Jim, Dale and I saw the Mck-Fees and their men talking outside the hotel's front door and had to escape through the back."

"The Mck-Fees were maintaining mobile phone contact with Radeski when they were pursuing us," Reynolds started off.

"Not only Radeski, but also the De Marco brothers," Bernardo continued.

"And that's how Radeski's people found us at the hotel," Reynolds concluded.

"It beats the hell out of me," Melissa remarked, her face frowning.

"But the Mck-Fees' gang has always been four or five miles behind us," Dave said. "And they always know which route we're taking, which town or village or district we're heading towards and which landmark we're stopping at. I got it!"

"You got it?" Jim asked.

"They put a tracking device on our van!" Dave exclaimed. "Probably underneath. That's how they've managed to follow our movements!"

"They must've placed it at the hospital in Chicago," Dale added.

"They knew that if me and Nicole were critically injured in that shootout outside the church, you'd have to run us to the hospital," Melissa told Dave. "So that was their next stop and when we were all inside, the Mck-Fees' thugs placed the device on our van."

"And then they had us followed," Dale said.

"And tracked us to the Lamenskis' country estate!" Dave snapped.

"And they're probably pursuing us now!" Jim exclaimed. "Five miles behind us, guys!"

"No, they're not," Dale remarked, his manner reassuring.

"Tell them what you did!" Melissa enthused.

"What was that?" Dave wanted to know.

"I immobilized the Mck-Fees' van," Dale said proudly.

"I pointed the handgun into each tire to muffle the gunshot, and I fired. All four tires on their vehicle are out of action. The Mck-Fees can't pursue us now."

"Yeah!" Reynolds and Bernardo yelled. "Good thinking!"

"It was good thinking, guys!" Melissa enthusiastically agreed. "My husband is amazing! Don't you think?"

"Sometimes I even surprise myself!" Dale called out.

"It was good thinking," Dave said. "You're a smart kid. As smart as that daredevil, Jim."

"I couldn't have done it better myself!" Jim cried. "The Mck-Fees can't pursue us now, but that's not the end of our troubles."

"How do you mean?" Dave asked.

"The tracking device," Jim replied. "We must find it and destroy it when we reach Akron. And now that the Mck-Fees know where the Lamenskis' country estate is positioned, the rest of their cartel in Chicago will be ready to attack. The Mck-Fees only have to make a call to their co-leaders in order for the thugs to pull the hit operation against the estate. You must contact the Lamenskis to warn them and Sam Ringwood's guys."

"I can't," Dave realized immediately. "They've disconnected their telephone. And I don't have their mobile phone number. Damn it!"

"Can you make a call to Sam or Toby?" Jim inquired.

"I don't know their numbers either!" Dave cried. "Only Nicole knew them."

"We left Nicole's phone inside her leather jacket at the Lamenskis' place," Jim said. "We must make the call to the Lamenskis via Nicole's mobile number."

"I got it," Dave agreed. He reached inside the pocket of his brown leather jacket and pulled out his own mobile before dialing Nicole's number. But there was no dial tone, meaning her phone was switched off. "Damn it!" Dave shouted.

"What is it?" Jim cried.

"Nicole's mobile is switched off!" Dave panicked.

"There's no way of getting through to the Lamenskis?" Dale inquired.

"This is serious!" Jim added.

"Sam's men and Toby will be sitting ducks," Dave said with a worried look on his face. "Only four cops against God knows how many mobsters. I don't think we're going to like the outcome, guys."

Within the next six minutes, Jim's vehicle reached Akron. Jim drove into a gas station for fuel before it halted and he switched off the ignition.

***

Within a mile of the Lamenskis' country estate, a black limousine and a truck approached each other on a country road. A mob of Mafia men and a woman, led by the De Francos, got out of the limo, while the rest of the Mck-Fee Cartel's thugs, under Paul Vaston and John Lumumber, emerged from the truck. Both heavily armed gangs approached each other in a menacing manner and came to a halt, brandishing their powerful high-velocity rifles with evil in their minds.

Part 4

Paul Vaston's mob faced the De Francos' gang with only ten feet of country road separating them.

The De Francos and their thugs were dressed in suits. One of the brothers was a medium-sized man with dark hair and a screwed-up face, and the other was a shorter guy with black hair and glasses. The other Mafia people included a well-built, brown-haired woman in a brown suit, a big stocky man with grey hair, a young man with brownish-fair hair, a guy with medium-length black hair and a hard, aggressive face, and another young man with fair hair.

Vaston was a tall, muscular Frenchman with dark hair and a hard, cold face. He was wearing jeans, a shirt and a gray overcoat, and the others in his mob were also dressed casually. John Lumumber was a bearded black man with long hair hanging down to his shoulders. Standing alongside them were two big, muscular white men with long brown hair and beards, another smaller guy with short dark hair, a mustache and a small beard on his chin, and four other medium-height, clean-shaven guys, three of them brown-haired and the fourth had black hair.

As the De Francos' thugs faced Vaston's, four more of Vaston's men sneaked up from their hiding places in a wheat field behind the limousine, then made their way to the limo and placed an explosive device under it, rigging the bomb to explode after ten minutes. These men included a rough, hard-faced man of thirty-two with short blond hair, another guy with long blond hair, a bearded man with long brownish-blond hair, and a middle-aged guy with medium-length dark hair. After placing the weapon, the thugs retreated back into the wheat field.

The De Francos hesitated before addressing Vaston and Lumumber.

"You wanted to see us," the brother with glasses began.

"Why is this?" the other brother asked.

"We know where the De Marco brothers are," Vaston told them, his voice slow and heavy. "They're in Pittsburgh. That's all I wanted to tell you."

"Then we will find them and kill them," the man with glasses said. "Thanks. I have some money to pay you for this information." He turned towards his brother and the rest of the mob. "Return to the limo."

The Mafia men and the woman made their way back to the enormous car and climbed inside as the brother with glasses opened a suitcase with ten thousand dollars inside. Then, suddenly, the whole atmosphere was ripped apart by a terrifying explosion, the force of the blast tearing the limousine to pieces and killing the other De Franco brother and all the Mafia thugs. The brother with glasses was transfixed with shock and horror. The four bombers emerged again from the wheat field and approached him from behind.

"Sorry, my friend," Vaston snarled coldly. "But the Mck-Fees vowed to protect the De Marco brothers."

Vaston aimed his rifle and blazed with a deafening gunshot, which echoed through the sky. The brother with glasses fell to the road, the center of his chest plastered with blood.

The thirteen thugs watched the burning car being eaten away by orange-yellow flames and billowing black smoke.

The Frenchman turned to his mobsters. "The estate is nearly a mile away to the east. It is that big house over there. Take the cash, climb into the truck and drive. We have work to do."

Vaston and Lumumber led the thugs back towards the truck.

***

Inside the country estate, Sam's men had slept during the afternoon and were now keeping watch for the night. Harry and Glenda had made coffees for Sam and Toby, but Carrouso, Goldblum and Glen had no wish to have drinks.

Sam and Toby heard a large vehicle stop outside the estate.

"You hear that?" Toby asked.

"I hear it," Sam saidted.

"It sounds like a truck," Glen pointed out.

"Are you expecting visitors, Harry, Glenda?" Goldblum wanted to know.

"No, we're not," Harry said.

"It's mighty strange," Glenda added.

"We'll check it out," Glen decided.

The cops approached the dining room window and spotted Vaston's rough-tough mobsters advancing down the drive, armed with high-velocity rifles.

"Oh my God, Mck-Fee's men!" Goldblum exclaimed.

"Harry, Glenda, go upstairs and lock yourselves in the bathroom!" Carrouso ordered.

"Go, now!" Goldblum yelled.

"Toby, you protect Nicole!" Sam commanded his son. "Here's one of my handguns, fully loaded." He passed the weapon to Toby.

"Okay, Dad," Toby replied. "Harry, Glenda, come with me."

Harry and Glenda raced upstairs and locked themselves in the bathroom. Toby followed them, then darted into Nicole's room and hid behind the open door.

"Are the burglar-alarm systems working?" Glen asked frantically.

"They've gone lousy!" Sam complained.

At that moment, a loud gunshot blasted through the night air, and the dining room window shattered. More shots came through the broken window.

"This is serious!" Carrouso yelled.

"We'll face them at the door!" Sam cried.

The cops focused their handguns towards the front door, waiting for Vaston's men to smash through. The dining room curtains were drawn, so there was no way the thugs would see the detectives entering the hallway to confront them. In the next second, Vaston's rifle blasted the front door's locks and chain, and then the four bombers who had booby-trapped the De Francos' limousine forced the door open and stormed in, followed by the remaining thugs. Sam fired three shots into one of the men, while Carrouso and Goldblum blazed five shots at two others and Glen sent two into the fourth thug's chest. All four brutes went down, blood pouring from their wounds. The detectives fled back into the dining room as the other mobsters fired savagely into the hallway. They slammed the door shut and dived behind a settee between the dinner table and the wine cabinet. Vaston and Lumumber smashed the door in, and all nine thugs showered the dining room with ferocious rifle fire, causing extreme destruction, mayhem and terror.

"Cover us," Vaston told the other seven thugs, then he and Lumumber raced up the stairs.

Out of range of the cops, who were still crouched behind the settee, the seven mobsters rained a vicious barrage of lethal gunfire throughout the room again. The bullets smashed the vases and wine cabinet, shredded the settee and armchairs to bits and made large holes in the walls.

Sam took the initiative, putting his own life in danger.

"Get ready!" he shouted to Carrouso, Goldblum and Glen.

He rolled behind the wine cabinet and then crouched on the floor and ruthlessly fired. Three shots killed the first mobster and then another four deadly blasts cut down a second, and both brutes crashed against the wall and crumpled awkwardly to the floor. Sam then retreated behind the cabinet, shouting, "Now!"

The five surviving drug dealers pumped a volley of ferocious gunfire towards the cabinet and the wall behind the armchairs and settee, while Carrouso, Goldblum and Glen reacted to Sam's order and blazed with their handguns. Carrouso cut down two men with five savage blasts, while Goldblum sent four rounds into the fifth dealer, and Glen dispatched the last two with five vicious shots. All five dealers fell to the floor alongside the two mobsters Sam had gunned down.

The floor and the wall were smeared crimson-red, and blood was spilling from the thugs' wounds. The four vice cops emerged from their hiding places and were shocked and appalled by the carnage. All of them were unnerved by how close they had come to being massacred by the fearsome mob who had outnumbered and outgunned them.

***

Toby stood tense behind the open bedroom door and clenched the handgun Sam had lent him. Although only a lawyer, Toby was a brave young man with the strength, courage and determination of his father; protecting Nicole was his responsibility. Lying unconscious in bed, she was extremely vulnerable, and whatever the odds, Toby was not about to let her down now.

In the next few seconds, petrifying Toby to breaking point, Vaston and Lumumber entered the bedroom and flicked on the light. They saw Nicole tucked up in bed, lying under the covers, and aimed their rifles towards her.

At that moment, Toby's terror became rage. He darted out from between the door and the wall, focused his gun on Lumumber's head and blazed. The swaggering brute tumbled to the floor, his head spewing blood. Vaston spun round furiously, his evil stare piercing into Toby's face. He aimed his rifle, but Toby rugby-tackled him, yelling, "You son of a bitch!"

With ferocious violence, both men crashed against the wall. They fought viciously over the rifle, but Vaston was much larger and stronger than Toby and he turned, pinning Toby against the wall. The barrel of Vaston's rifle was close to Toby's neck, ready to blow his head off, but Toby instinctively swung his left arm round, pushing it away, and then kicked hard at Vaston's shin. Vaston cried out with pain, and Toby took the opportunity to crash his knee up against Vaston's groin so that the hardened thug cried out again and doubled up in agony, clutching his privates. Toby grabbed the rifle and smashed the butt against Vaston's face with two vicious blows, hurtling the ruthless dealer backwards towards the bed. He then spun the weapon round, aimed it at the Frenchman's chest and squeezed the trigger. Two roaring blasts ruptured Vaston's chest, and he slumped to the floor, ugly rivers of blood coming out of his entry and exit wounds and staining the bed and the carpet.

Toby breathed heavily. He had never been so terrified, not even in Miami's harbor nine years ago where he had killed the drug dealer Rick Schneider who had been complicit in Nicole's kidnapping and attempted rape. Toby had protected Nicole again, but he didn't feel like a hero. He had killed two more men, and next to terror, he felt remorse and sorrow.

Sam, Carrouso and Goldblum came into the bedroom.

"Are you okay, son?" Sam asked.

"I'm okay, Dad," Toby sighed. "Just okay."

Sam placed his hand on Toby's shoulder, proudly.

"It must've been hard for you," Sam reassured him. "But you did great, son."

"I know," Toby replied painfully.

Then, Glenda, Harry and Glen came into the room. Glenda was sobbing and Harry comforted her, holding her to his chest.

Sam and Toby collapsed onto the bed, adrenalin running viciously through their bodies. After a few moments, they relaxed.

"The mob know we're here," Carrouso told Sam.

"Shall we call for more cops?" Goldblum asked.

"It would be wise," Glen added.

"Yeah, do it," Sam growled, his harsh voice tired.

Carrouso, Goldblum and Glen left to make the call.

"Is Nicole okay?" Harry asked.

"She's okay," Toby replied.

"Toby saved her life," Sam reported gently.

"We owe you and your father's detectives a mountain of respect for protecting Nicole and the two of us," Glenda thanked him.

"Think nothing of it," Toby told her.

The four of them sat with Nicole, waiting for the uniforms plus the CSI and Forensics people to arrive on the scene.

***

At Akron, while Jim pumped gasoline into the squad van's fuel tank, the others searched for the tracking device. Dale combed through the engine compartment, Reynolds and Bernardo looked behind and underneath the seats, and Dave and Melissa searched under the van and between the tires.

"You found anything, Dale?" Jim wanted to know.

"No, but it must be here somewhere," Dale said.

"Keep looking," Jim insisted. He addressed Reynolds and Bernardo. "You found the device, guys?"

"No," Reynolds replied. "It ain't inside the vehicle, Jim."

"It must be underneath the van, señor," Bernardo decided.

"That's the best hiding place for a tracking device," Dave said.

"But we haven't had any luck finding it," Melissa said.

"Well, keep looking," Jim ordered.

"How's your arm, Melissa?" Dave inquired. "You've removed your sling."

"My arm's getting much better," Melissa said, grinning. "There's much less pain."

"I'm glad to hear that," Dale said.

"But don't put too much strain on your arm," Reynolds advised her.

"I'm not an invalid," Melissa objected, her face frowning.

"No, you're not, honey," Dale agreed. "But any time you want to rest, let me take over. The device is not under the hood."

"There's one place we haven't looked," Dave said.

"Yeah? Fill me in," Melissa insisted, her voice excited.

"Fill us in, Melissa," Dale protested. "There's six of us here."

"We're dying to know," Jim added ruggedly.

"The brakes," Dave indicated. "We haven't searched the brakes."

He eased his way towards where the brakes were positioned, and his hand felt a hard, square object. He pulled it away, and his hand emerged from this small, enclosed area holding the tracking device.

"You found it!" Melissa screamed with joy.

Dave emerged from underneath the vehicle. "One tracking device coming right up," he said.

"You never cease to amaze me, kid," Jim informed the young Quaker.

"Don't call me kid anymore," Dave complained. "I'm forty now, despite my blond hair and youthful appearance."

"Sorry pal, that's just my way."

"You know how patronizing Jim can be," Dale remarked lightly.

"We know all too well, señor," Bernardo joked.

"What do we do with the device now?" Reynolds said.

"We destroy it," Jim answered casually.

"I found it, so I should destroy it," Dave pointed out. "But I'll leave it to Melissa."

"Thank you," Melissa enthused, grinning shyly.

Dave and Melissa rose to their feet, and Melissa forcefully smashed the tracking device with her shoe. She brought it off the ground and dumped it inside a garbage can.

"The device is no more, Dave, Jim, Dale." Melissa kissed Dave's cheek playfully and then kissed Dale's lips. "What do we do now, guys?"

"I've filled the gas tank," Jim said.

"I'm dying to eat those pizzas," Dave suggested. "We can share one between three."

"That's a cool idea," Reynolds agreed.

"We'll share our pizza with Jim," Bernardo decided.

"I'll buy six cans of American beer or lager," Jim said.

"How about you buy me a can of lemonade?" Dave asked. "I'll take over the driving from now on. Buy one lemonade and five beers or lagers."

"It is done," Jim replied.

"I'll share a pizza with Dale and Melissa," Dave decided. "Two boxes of pizza coming right up."

"I'll pay for the fuel, buy the cans of drink and we'll be off," Jim said with a laugh. "You guys keep a lookout for any unwanted company."

"They won't get far with flat tires." Dave chuckled and smiled at Dale with admiration.

***

Inside the Mck-Fees' van outside the saloon, Matt and Ray saw the tracking indicator on their computer fade into nothing.

"They've found the tracking device!" Matt snarled. "And destroyed it!"

"Now we'll never find them," Ray growled.

"But wait," Matt hissed. "They were heading for Akron. You know why, Ray?"

"Tell me!" Ray demanded.

"Akron is on the way to Pittsburgh!" Matt began. "Manuchi's former house, Maple Lodge, is on the southern outskirts of Pittsburgh, in Aspen Avenue.

"I have a hunch the Timlook detectives will visit Manuchi's place to have coffees and a bite to eat. Now that the De Marco brothers, John Hazinski and Miles Carter live in Pittsburgh—Miles Carter is an explosive expert!—I'll give them a call and order Carter to break into Maple Lodge and booby-trap the place. If Manuchi has a car parked there, he can booby-trap the car as well. Both explosive devices will have a delayed detonation of ten minutes, giving the cops plenty of time to gather inside the house or hang about outside close to the car."

"It'll be a piece of cake, Matt," Ray sneered sadistically.

"While we wait for roadside assistance to replace our tires," Matt continued. "I'll phone the De Marco brothers." His hand went into his leather jacket and produced his mobile, then dialed

Miles Carter's telephone number. There were five bleeps, and then a rough-voiced answer.

"Hi there, it's Miles Carter here, who's calling?" The following conversation took five minutes.

***

John Hazinski waited outside the open door of Maple Lodge, keeping watch, as Miles Carter set an explosive device in a kitchen cupboard. Carter also set a tripwire, which was well-hidden in the thick carpet leading into the kitchen, hiding the excess underneath two mats and between two boxes of Polish beer. When one of the detectives walked through the hallway into the kitchen, he or she would tread on the wire, and the pressure would pull the pin out of the device. The bomb would tick for ten minutes, allowing all the detectives plenty of time to gather inside Maple Lodge, and at the end of the delayed reaction time, the resulting explosion would kill them all. Planting the device and the tripwire took twenty minutes, then Carter came out of the front door and shut it securely.

"How did it go, Miles?" Hazinski wanted to know.

"The works," Carter sneered. "Now to set the second bomb inside Dale Manuchi's old car, in case they don't make themselves at home inside. They may decide to take his car somewhere instead, but again, the delayed reaction will be ten minutes."

It took fifteen minutes for Carter to set up the device under the hood so that the pin would be pulled by the engine starting. Hazinski maintained vigilance.

***

As Jim's van reached the Ohio-Pennsylvania border, the detectives could see a fortress of mountains leading onto the Allegheny Plateau, which then led down to the Piedmont Plateau. These were the Appalachian Mountains separating the eastern United States from the vast prairies. Within five minutes, the van was ascending a mountain road.

"Aren't the Appalachian Mountains beautiful?" Dale enthused.

"They sure are," Melissa agreed.

"We're approaching forests in these mountains," Bernardo observed.

"They are as thick as those in the Amazon," Reynolds said with a laugh.

"You'd better believe it, guys," Jim said.

"We're approaching Pittsburgh," Dale added. "There's no food or drinks in the house; we haven't visited the place for two weeks."

"We must give Captain Merson a call," Dave said.

***

Having driven down Aspen Avenue, Dave pulled the squad van into the driveway of Maple Lodge and pulled up between Dale's old car and the garden. Opening the rear doors, Dale, Melissa, Reynolds and Bernardo climbed out, while Dave and Jim vacated the front seats and slammed the doors shut. Dale reached inside his brown leather jacket for a set of skeleton keys, twisted one into the front door of the house and yanked it open. The cops made their way inside and Jim, Melissa, Reynolds and Bernardo congregated in the dining room.

Dave and Dale walked casually towards the kitchen, and Dave unknowingly trod on the tripwire hidden in the hallway's thick carpet. The pin slipped out of the explosive device inside the kitchen cupboard and its digital clock began the ten-minute countdown.

"I must use your phone, Dale," Dave said.

"Go ahead," Dale agreed.

They stood together in the hallway as Dave dialed the number for Timlook PD. There were five bleeps before Captain Merson answered the call.

"Hi there, Timlook Police Department, Captain Robert Merson here. How can I help you?"

"Captain, it's me Dave," the young Quaker began. "I'm calling from Dale's former house in Pittsburgh. We've been on a long journey from Chicago, and we'll be in Timlook shortly."

"What happened to you guys, Dave?" Captain Merson asked, his voice rough. "I heard there was a shootout outside the Christian church in Chicago. The Illinois Branch of the FBI phoned my department to inform me, and they told me the court cases against the four drug cartels were off."

"I can explain, Captain," Dave suggested.

"Go on, I must hear the not-so-pleasant news," Merson said.

"There was a second shootout in which Chief Renko, eight uniforms, and Detectives Lopez

Carreras and Clara Brown were killed. Nicole was critically injured and may not survive." Dave paused for a moment to regain his composure. "Squad Leader Sam Ringwood, his remaining vice cops and his son Toby are protecting Nicole," he continued. "But my worst fear is that the Mck-Fees' mob in Chicago have got to them.

"Melissa was also shot and injured in the shootout, but is recovering well, and she, Dale and me have been driving all the way from Chicago, accompanied by Jim, Reynolds and Bernardo. We're safe at Dale's place in Pittsburgh now. I'll tell you more news when we've returned to Timlook."

"Where are the Mck-Fees now?" Merson wanted to know.

"They had been pursuing us in their van," Dave said. "But we've left them far behind. Listen, I must go now."

"Okay, hang in there," Merson said. "Good day."

"Good day, Captain," Dave said. He replaced the phone.

"What now, Dave?" Dale inquired.

"I must get a drink of water from your faucet," Dave decided.

"Go ahead," Dale invited him.

As Dave entered the kitchen, his foot accidentally knocked one of the two boxes of Polish beer at an angle, and he spotted the tripwire.

"Jim! Dale!" Dave exclaimed. "I see a wire!"

"A wire?" Jim replied frantically.

"Damn it, you're right!" Dale snapped. "That wasn't there when we last stayed here."

"It's a tripwire!" Dave panicked. "The mob have been here!" He yanked open the kitchen cupboard doors.

The detectives spotted the bomb in a bottom cupboard, the pin at the end of the wire lying in front of it, and the digital clock indicating only thirty seconds left until detonation. A chilling spasm of terror gripped them.

"It's a bomb!" Dave cried. "Everybody, get out of the building! This whole place is about to blow!"

The detectives hurried out of the kitchen, down the hallway, through the dining room and pulled open the front door. They sprinted into the garden and dove for the grass, curling their legs, arms and heads up under their upper bodies and covering their ears with their hands.

The whole of Maple Lodge was gutted by a terrifying explosion, the sheer ferocious force of the blast sending wood, metal and glass flying onto the driveway and garden, narrowly missing the detectives, and smashing the metal frames, doors and windows of Dale's old car and the squad van, making both vehicles useless to drive in. A massive chunk of wood landed on the car's bonnet and not only caused the pin on the tripwire to slip out of the second bomb, but shook the device's mixture of dynamite and Semtex violently. The bomb exploded powerfully, ripping the car to pieces and completing the merciless destruction of Jim's van. The flames leapt savagely into the air, consuming the house, the car and the van.

The cops suffered several minutes of shellshock and horror before Melissa began whimpering and Dale was overcome by insane rage.

"They've been in my house!" Dale yelled. "And now the house, the car and the van are destroyed! Jesus Christ!"

"Dale, please don't lose your cool," Melissa begged him as she fought back tears, her body shaking. "I know you're mad, but keep your head together for me, please. I'm scared, my body is trembling and my legs are like jelly, but I'm trying to stay strong for everybody. I need you right now, the way you need me. Don't give up on me. Or everybody else. Please, Dale." She was breathing heavily and tears soaked her face.

Dale held her protectively in an embrace and clutched her arms tightly.

"I'm not giving up on you, Melissa," Dale promised as he calmed down. "Or anybody else. I'm your husband and I care about you. We'll all see this through to the bitter end. Don't worry, honey."

"In any case," Dave began, his voice sensitive, "cops help each other out and pull together when a fellow cop is in danger. The Mck-Fees only want you dead, but we'll all stick by you through thick and thin. So don't worry, Melissa."

"These guys really know what they're doing," Dale snapped. "They're not amateurs. Wherever we run, they'll find us. They mean business."

"These guys are serious," Jim agreed, his face gripped by terror.

"What's that piece of leather I see in the flowerbed?" Dave observed. "A wallet. Is that your wallet, Dale, Melissa?"

"No, Dave," Dale replied.

"It's not mine," Melissa remarked, her face and forehead frowning.

Jim, Reynolds and Bernardo also denied ownership.

"And it sure ain't mine," Dave commented. He crawled over towards the flowerbed, yanked the leather wallet away from the flowers and opened it to find an ID card. "Miles Carter," Dave said. "A rough-looking, bearded man in his thirties with long, blond hair, who lives at twenty-four Oak Lane, South Pittsburgh. I'm guessing he planted the devices and his wallet must've accidentally fallen out of his pocket."

"South Pittsburgh, that's only half a mile from here," Dale informed the others. "I lived in Pittsburgh for seven years, so I know. We're in south-east Pittsburgh, so we must double back towards Oak Lane and confirm that this is one of the bastards who blew up my house."

"Before the Mck-Fees find us," Bernardo remarked.

"Half a mile?" Reynolds asked. "That's only ten to fifteen minutes' walk away from here."

"That's if we run, not walk," Jim replied.

"Or jog," Melissa pointed out. "But once we've nailed the bomber and his gang, and phoned the Pittsburgh PD in order for the police to pick them up, how will we return to Timlook?"

"Good question," Dale said. "My car and our van are now useless."

"Any ideas, people?" Jim inquired.

"We take the first morning train to Timlook," Dave decided.

"We visited Pittsburgh two weeks ago," Dale pointed out, "and I remember reading my own train timetable. The first train to Timlook is at five-fifty a.m. It's now four a.m., meaning we have an hour and fifty minutes. We'll use the next hour to bust and detain the bomber and his gang, gather more information and call the police, then the following fifty minutes to take their car and drive to the station."

"Let's go," Dave ordered.

The detectives abandoned Dale's burning house, and doubled back towards Oak Lane, maintaining a steady jog.

***

The detectives sneaked their way under the barbed wire fence which closed off the back gardens of Twenty-four Oak Lane. On the vast lawn was positioned a military helicopter with 'De Marco Brothers' painted on both sides.

"De Marco brothers," Dave whispered. "They own that helicopter. You remember that missile attack on the Chicago-Toledo highway? When we heard the terrible news on the squad van's radio, witnesses told reporters they saw 'De Marco Brothers' painted on the helicopter that carried out the attack. So, after that Mafia gang in Chicago, headed by the De Marcos, was massacred by the De Francos' mob, the De Marcos must have fled to Pittsburgh under the Mck-Fees' protection, and are now seeking refuge with this Miles Carter."

"Look over there, either side of the mass of thickets in the center of the gardens," Jim pointed out.

"Two groups of armed men," Dale added.

"One group are guarding the helicopter," Dave said, "and the second group are patrolling the other side of the thickets. They have their backs to us. We'll have to kill these guys, which will alert the De Marcos, so we'll have to kill them and Carter as well. Let's sneak towards the thickets now, while both groups of gunmen are facing the other way."

Dave's detectives crawled up from under the wire fence, rose to their feet, pulled out their handguns and sprinted towards the east side of the thickets where the first group of gunmen were patrolling. The group consisted of five Mexicans, all with beards or mustaches, and two bearded Americans, all casually dressed. All were violent, rough-tough brutes who had murdered several cops with their sub-machine guns.

The detectives were outnumbered and outgunned by these hardened thugs, and as soon as the seven gunmen turned and saw the detectives heading towards them, Dave's team dove for the grass and opened fire. The gunmen sprayed bullets over the detectives' heads, but Reynolds and Bernardo fired nine shots into the two Americans, who hurtled to the grass. Reynolds and Bernardo were out of ammunition, but Dale and Melissa blazed with six gunshots each and brought down two of the Mexicans. Dave felled a third Mexican with two shots and then dropped the fourth man with three blasts, while Jim pumped five rounds viciously into the fifth. All seven gunmen were sprawled in an undignified manner on the grass, their wounds streaming blood.

The second group of four rough-looking Mexicans abandoned the helicopter on the west side of the thickets, hurried round the north side and made their way behind the detectives. Without ammunition, Reynolds and Bernardo were totally defenseless, but Dave, Jim, Dale and Melissa rolled onto their backs, focused their handguns towards the Mexicans and opened fire. Dale sent five blasts and Melissa pumped another four into two Mexicans, the gunmen falling awkwardly to the grass. Dave hit the third gunman with six exploding shots, while Jim blazed with five fierce blasts towards the fourth, and both gunmen went down in seconds, blood running freely from their injuries and soaking their chests.

"The De Marcos will have been alerted by the gunfire," Dave cried.

"Reynolds, Bernardo and Melissa, you go round the front to cut off their escape," Jim ordered. "Myself, Dave and Dale will break in through the kitchen door."

"We've reloaded," Reynolds shouted.

"Then let's go, señor," Bernardo said.

"I'm right behind you," Melissa asserted.

The detectives covered the distance from the thickets to the kitchen door in only five seconds, and as Melissa, Reynolds and Bernardo hurried round the front to guard the mobsters' two cars parked in the driveway, Dave, Jim and Dale smashed their weight against the kitchen door and stormed inside. They darted through the kitchen and dived behind the settee as they were met with a ferocious hail of deafening gunfire exploding from three rifles held by John Hazinski and the De Marco brothers. The savage bombardment shredded the settee and armchairs to ribbons, but Dale rolled back into the kitchen, focused his handgun, and the weapon vomited two violent shots into Hazinski's chest. The big, mustached brute crashed against the wall and fell forwards to the floor, but the De Marcos then blasted towards Dale as he retreated further into the kitchen.

The distraction worked to Dave's advantage, and he and Jim popped up above the settee, trained their handguns and sent a series of shots exploding from their weaponry. Three blasts from Jim's piece pumped hot lead bullets into one of the De Marcos, rupturing his heart, and four shots from Dave's weapon punctured the other brother's lungs and pancreas, and both brothers hit the wall with sickening impact and slumped to the floor.

"That's put paid to these guys," Dave said.

"But where's Miles Carter?" Jim inquired.

"He must be hiding somewhere," Dale snapped.

At that moment, Reynolds and Bernardo forced the front door in and charged into the house, focusing their handguns.

"It's okay guys, you're too late," Jim said.

"We heard shooting," Reynolds snarled.

"You've brought down the De Marco brothers and a third guy," Bernardo observed.

"His name's John Hazinski," Reynolds told him.

"John Hazinski?" Jim asked.

"He was the De Marco brothers' financial advisor and he kept records of crooked deals the Mck-Fees cut with the other drug cartels," Dave informed his team. "The Pittsburgh police ran an investigation into Hazinski a year ago under suspicion of money laundering, extortion and passing money, drugs and weapons between the cartels. They obtained his file with the list of cartels inside the New England Net, and all the corrupt deals, murders and hit operations the cartels were behind, but the file was stolen and never recovered. It was the De Marcos and Miles Carter who were behind the missing file."

"It must be somewhere around here," Dale said.

"We have to find it," Jim added.

"And keep our eyes open for Miles Carter," Dave told the others.

"We'll head upstairs," Reynolds said.

"No, we'll search the room next door," Bernardo insisted.

"I'll search upstairs," Jim added lightly.

"And I'll ferret through the dining room," Dave said.

"Where's Melissa?" Dale wondered.

"Hunting for Miles Carter," Bernardo replied.

"I'll search for her," Dale said.

Jim, Reynolds and Bernardo left the room, Jim making his way upstairs.

"Dale, check that Melissa's okay when you find her," Dave said.

"I will, Dave," Dale agreed.

As Dave rummaged through the drawers in the dining room, Dale entered the kitchen and began to look for Melissa, before hearing movement outside. The young detective focused his handgun through the kitchen door as the noise of running footsteps came his way. He walked cautiously through the door and into the garden, and then Melissa emerged from around the front yard, staring with petrified terror into his face, and trained her handgun in his direction.

"Drop to the ground!" she cried.

Melissa ran towards Dale, her face and eyes contorted with concentration. Dale dropped down just as the long-haired, bearded Miles Carter fired a deadly blast from his rifle. It missed. The bullet whizzed past Melissa and punched a hole into the wall behind her. She aimed her handgun again and fired three vicious and deafening gunshots into Carter. The explosives expert hurtled back into an open boiler cupboard, crashed against the boiler and dropped awkwardly to the floor, his chest covered in blood.

Melissa raced towards Dale as he got up off the ground.

Part 5

Dave, Reynolds and Bernardo came running into the kitchen. Dale and Melissa also entered the room, and the cops stood rigidly over Miles Carter's body.

"Thanks, Melissa, I owe you one." Dale thanked his wife.

Her teeth and face were clenched with fear, and Dave and Dale were also terrified by how close Carter had come to killing Dale with his rifle.

"You're lucky I came round the corner in the nick of time," Melissa told him.

"The explosives expert, Miles Carter," Dave pointed out.

"The guy who booby-trapped my house and my car," Dale added.

"There's something else," Reynolds said.

"I hope you're about to tell us," Bernardo replied.

"We've found no sign of the missing file."

"A missing file?" Melissa exclaimed, her voice shocked.

"An incriminating file containing records of criminal activities," Dave said.

"I've got it," Jim called, returning from upstairs.

"The file?" Dave cried.

"This better be good," Melissa enthused, grinning.

"Hear this, guys," Jim said. "The first few pages contain all the criminal activities of the De

Marco brothers after their branch of the Mafia was massacred by the De Francos, as well as the activities of the Mck-Fee Cartel and the network forming the New England Net, including weapons purchases.

"It looks like the Mck-Fees blackmailed the De Marcos by threatening to expose their hideouts in Pittsburgh and Toledo to the De Francos. Giving in to blackmail, the De Marcos, with Hazinski and Carter, flew their helicopter out of Toledo and attacked the Chicago-Toledo highway, purposefully cutting off our route to Toledo."

"So we would divert to Detroit," Bernardo added.

"And run into Radeski's guys," Reynolds said.

"While the Mck-Fees backed them up," Dave said.

"That's not all," Jim continued.

"We're all ears," Dale said.

"In return for the De Marcos' helicopter attack, the Mck-Fees agreed to send their thugs, led by Paul Vaston and John Lumumber, to massacre the De Francos."

"The same guys who would attack the Lamenskis' place," Dave said.

"But there's no record of whether Vaston's men did actually confront the De Francos' mob, who came out on top, or whether they hit the Lamenskis' place," Jim finished.

"The De Marcos never heard back from Vaston or Lumumber," Dave informed Jim. "Maybe the dealers and the De Francos massacred each other. Or, maybe the Chicago police nailed them all before they could slaughter each other. Or, maybe the dealers killed the De Francos and their mob, then pulled the hit against the Lamenskis' place, but were foiled by Sam Ringwood's Miami vice cops. But, if that were the case, why wouldn't Sam, Toby or the Lamenskis make a call to us to tell us they were okay? We probably just don't know each other's numbers."

"It's a long shot anyway," Jim told Dave. "On this next page is a list of drug cartels from Chicago to Boston run by the Mck-Fee Cartel. They include Sean Radeski, Keith Bergman and Patrick Pilski in Detroit, the De Marcos in Toledo and Pittsburgh, Patrick Miller in Cleveland, Enrique Garibaldy and Klaus Richmann in Philadelphia, Jose Cortez and Juan Pazerra in New York, Jeff Tate in Boston and Jack Fallon in Timlook.

"There's a briefcase over there by the armchair. We'll slip this file into the case, take it with us on the Pittsburgh-Timlook train and display this evidence to Captain Merson at Timlook PD. He'll phone the police departments in these cities, and they'll pull a series of sting operations against the cartels. There'll be nowhere left for the Mck-Fees and their mob to hide, and all we'll have to worry about are the gang pursuing us to Timlook and the local cartel run by Jack Fallon. We'll hire Richard Kanaris's men and the FBI to handle Fallon."

"Are the addresses and phone numbers of the cartels mentioned?" Dale wanted to know. "So the police forces can find them fast."

"They're written down beside the cartels' names," Jim told everybody.

"Good work, Jim," Dave said.

"What's the time?" Melissa asked. "We must catch that train."

"My watch says five-ten a.m.," Jim said. We have forty minutes to get to the station."

"The mobsters have two cars parked in the driveway," Dave told Jim. "We'll take the cars, drive to the station, have a light breakfast and then board the train."

"Or eat on the train," Jim suggested. "We'll have more choices of food."

"Okay," Dave said. He grabbed the incriminating file from Jim's hands, slipped it into the briefcase and then approached the front door.

Dave pulled open the door, and the detectives left the house, shut the door behind them and then entered the two cars. Dale climbed into the driver's seat of the car in front, and Reynolds and Bernardo got in the back. Jim would follow in the car behind, with Dave and Melissa sitting behind him. Jim and Dale thrust their keys into the ignitions, kicked the accelerators and the vehicles raced towards the station.

***

Having arrived at five twenty-five a.m., the detectives vacated the vehicles and hurried towards the ticket office.

"Can you all afford train tickets?" Jim asked.

"No, we can't," Reynolds realized. "Bernardo and I are thirty dollars short."

"Dale and I are running low too," Melissa replied innocently.

"Give Jim and me all you have, and we'll pay the difference," Dave offered them. "We're rolling in bucks."

The six cops pooled their money to buy the tickets.

"We'll wait on the platform," Bernardo said.

The others headed towards the platform, while Dave and Jim pressed the bell and brought over the ticket inspector.

"Six tickets to Timlook," Jim said ruggedly.

***

At five-fifty a.m., the train came to a stop at Pittsburgh Station, and the detectives rose from the platform bench.

"Come on then," Dave said. "We'll get on now."

They wrenched open one of the doors and entered. It was another two minutes before they left the station.

The speeding train advanced east through the Appalachians.

The beaming sun was on the horizon by the time the train left the towering mountains behind and descended towards the meadows, pastures and woodlands of the Piedmont Plateau. The lush fields and green forests, typical of New England, resounded with the bleating of sheep and goats, the singing of birds, the hooves of horses pulling carts and buggies, which carried Amish families between their communities, and the deafening noise of the train.

Dave, Jim, Dale and Melissa sat around one table, while Reynolds and Bernardo sat at a table opposite. Melissa admired the rolling fields of Pennsylvania.

"The countryside is so beautiful," she commented to Dave and Dale. "There is only one area of America more beautiful than New England, and that's the Rockies. There's also cool countryside where I once lived with my parents near San Francisco. I was brought up as a farm girl on a ranch. I have long-distant memories of California, but I love the Rockies and New England even more. I'm a Goddamn country woman."

"You're right, New England is so beautiful," Dale enthused. "The countryside is similar to the real England the other side of the ocean, where we went on our honeymoon. And New England has a turbulent history.

"First the Pilgrim Fathers, then the Seven Years War between Great Britain and France, then the War of Independence and then the Civil War. And the colonists lived side by side with the native Americans, while the Amish came here from Switzerland. You see those Amish buggies?"

"I see them," Melissa replied.

"What about the Shakers and the Quakers?" Dave added. "Don't forget the Quakers. I'm a Quaker myself."

"Sorry Dave," Dale said.

"Morning has come, and I'm hungry," Jim interrupted. "What about you, Reynolds and Bernardo?"

"You're damn right we are," Bernardo said. "I'm so hungry I could eat an elephant."

"So am I, Jim," Reynolds enthused. "All this traveling has given me a real appetite."

"I could devour a nice, big pizza," Melissa said with a chuckle, smiling shyly. "With plenty of cheese and everything on it. And then a glass of root beer."

"I don't think they serve pizza," Jim said jokingly. "Pizza is not breakfast. But they probably serve root beer. Dave and I will run to the café car and get some food."

"The breakfast trolley is coming now, and you know what, they're serving banoffee pie," Dave said with a wink to Melissa.

"You know I don't like banoffee pie," Melissa whined playfully. "I'll have an apple pie with a bar of Belgian chocolate and a large glass of root beer."

Dave was shocked by Melissa's order of junk food, being a health-food fanatic himself, and he grimaced unashamedly. Melissa's bright smile broke across her face, and Jim and Dale chuckled.

"Okay, have it your way," Dave said. "Come on Jim, let's get some real breakfast."

The trolley stopped between the two tables, and the detectives fired their orders.

***

At Timlook PD, Dave spent two hours recounting to Captain Merson the chain of events leading from the shootout outside the church in Chicago to the train journey through Pennsylvania.

"I'm sorry about Nicole Lamenski," Merson said. "And about Lopez Carreras and Clara Brown."

"It doesn't look like Nicole will make it," Dave told him.

At that moment, Jim and Dale arrived at the office door.

"Come in," Merson invited the detectives. "What is it?"

Jim pushed open the door and they both entered.

"Jim has the incriminating file for you," Dale informed the captain.

"Here it is," Jim told him. "There's enough evidence in there to hang the drug cartels for good."

"Good work, Bradley, Mitchell, Manuchi," Merson praised them.

"It contains a whole list of crooked deals, murders and hit operations, and which cartels were responsible," Dave added, pride and confidence in his voice. "I must request you phone or email all the police departments in Chicago, Cleveland, Philadelphia, New York and Boston to give the go-ahead to pull sting operations against the remaining drug cartels. We should begin in Chicago and New York, so the Mck-Fees have no hideout to return to and the Cortez-Pazerra Cartel are immobilized, and then work our way down the network. In the meantime, you might order Richard Kanaris's vice squad and the FBI to pull an operation against Jack Fallon's cartel building."

"I'll send emails to these departments now," Merson replied. "And Kanaris's guys and the FBI will hit Fallon's building.

"You three, along with Morgan, Reynolds and Ruiz, must spend the next few days at Morgan's farmstead and relax. In the next few days, three FBI agents, Neil Green, Liam White and Tim Nelson, will join you to bolster your security."

"Thanks, Captain," Dave finished off.

Dave, Jim and Dale vacated the office and approached Melissa, Reynolds and Bernardo to tell them the plan.

***

Above New York's Bronx district, several police helicopters advanced, and the cartel building came into view. On the ground, groups of squad cars and vans full of uniforms and Feds were on route, speeding along the highway. Cortez's private army was on the roof, all fifteen thugs aiming their rifles towards the helicopters.

A terrifying barrage of gunfire charged and echoed through the atmosphere, but the helicopters were well-protected by bulletproof glass and not a single cop was hit.

The machines descended onto the roof before the uniforms stooped into lying-down positions, with their rifles aimed towards the mobsters, then opened fire. The lethal hail of rifle fire caused a deafening racket, which alerted Cortez and Pazerra inside the building, along with the two Mexicans, two Cubans and two Americans who were their bodyguards. As the thugs on the roof were massacred, the eight men leapt out of a back window, dropping down from the second floor, and sprinted towards Cortez's private helicopter They opened the side doors and scrambled inside; Cortez and Pazerra took the controls.

The squad cars and vans surrounded the building, and the uniforms and FBI people raced out of the vehicles, forced in the building's doors and darted inside in pursuit of the escaping dealers. But the helicopter rose into the air and veered round above the car park before flying away from the Bronx, out of New York and towards Pennsylvania.

"That was a close shave," Cortez shouted.

"Now, Timlook," Pazerra said.

***

Outside Jack Fallon's cartel building in North Timlook's Warsaw Street, Kanaris's detectives, Mark Blondel and a team of Feds left their vehicles and covered all the building's doors. Rubbing his own beard, Kanaris gave the signal for the Feds to force in the doors.

Ramming their combined weight against the doors, the Feds stormed inside, followed by vice cops Kanaris, Jan, Felt, Felder and Blondel.

"On the floor, all of you!" Kanaris and Jan shouted.

"Spread your limbs, now!" Felt, Felder and Blondel cried violently. The vice cops restrained five dealers and handcuffed them while the Feds cornered Fallon and his remaining thugs. As the FBI men manhandled the handcuffed dealers into their vans, Kanaris's men spotted two thugs escaping through a back window.

"Freeze, or we'll shoot!" Blondel called.

The vice cops blazed towards the window, but missed.

"After them, guys!" Kanaris cried.

Darting towards the window, they were too late as the two drug dealers in suits fled down the alleyway. The hippy cops held their fire.

"You got a good look at them?" Felt snapped.

"I did," Jan replied. "Both were clean-shaven and wore black suits."

"One was tall with brown hair," Felder told Felt.

"And the other of medium height with blond hair," Blondel explained. "Did you see their faces?"

"None of us did," Felt told Blondel.

"Jack Fallon's guys will tough it out in the department's jail cell," Kanaris decided. "We'll spend the rest of the day guarding Jim's detectives at Dale and Melissa's farmstead, waiting for FBI agents Green, White and Nelson to arrive. Then we'll ruthlessly interrogate Fallon until he gives us the names of those two thugs in suits, for I'm determined to nail these guys."

***

At the Lamenskis' country estate outside Chicago, a team of uniforms stood guard as two teams of CSI and Forensics identified the bodies of Paul Vaston's men.

One Forensics guy told Sam and Toby two crucial pieces of information connected to the dead thugs. First, that the De Francos' mob was found massacred on a country lane nearby, with most of the victims lying in and around a burned-out limousine, and the elder De Franco brother sprawled with a gunshot wound to his chest. Sam and Toby knew the thugs led by Vaston and Lumumber were behind the hit. Secondly, that when Chicago Homicide and the FBI pulled the sting operation against the Mck-Fees' cartel building, they discovered the hideout empty. Sam knew this was due partly to the first gang being out pursuing Dave's Homicide detectives to Timlook, and also to the second gang, under Vaston and Lumumber, having already been dispatched by the vice cops and Toby in their vain attempt to murder everyone at the estate.

"You thinking what I'm thinking, Dad?" Toby asked Sam.

"About what?" Sam wanted to know.

"How Chicago Homicide and the FBI found the location of the Mck-Fees' cartel building in the first place," Toby answered.

"You tell me," Sam invited the young lawyer.

"Timlook PD must have sent emails to other departments containing the addresses of drug cartels from Chicago and Detroit to Philadelphia, New York and Boston," Toby explained. "I heard on the news several cartels have been busted. And that's not all."

"Tell me more," Sam said.

"The Cortez-Pazerra Cartel building in New York has been hit."

"So we no longer have to worry about Juan Pazerra?"

"Don't cross your fingers yet," Toby warned. "Fifteen Mexicans died in a shootout with the helicopter police on the building's rooftop, but Pazerra, Cortez, two Mexicans, two Cubans and two Americans escaped in Cortez's chopper and flew out of New York. We must still watch our backs. You follow?"

"Looks real bad," Sam replied.

Harry and Glenda came out of the house's front door, Glenda carrying two glasses of lemonade.

"You two fancy lemonades?" Harry asked.

"Whilst we check on Nicole," Glenda explained.

"Carrouso, Goldblum and Hawke are watching over her," Sam said.

"Let's all join them," Toby decided.

They entered the building, made their way past the CSI and Forensics men and headed upstairs.

***

Carrouso, Goldblum and Glen sat around Nicole's bed.

"She's beginning to breathe more heavily," Glen said. He massaged his own mustache. "I'll check her pulse." Glen pressed his fingers against Nicole's neck, then felt her wrist. "Her pulse is strengthening!" Glen exclaimed.

"You're joking!" Goldblum said, full of hope.

Nicole began to hum and mumble in her sleep, and her forehead creased up. She turned her head on her long brunette hair, and her chin touched the pillow.

"Sam, Toby!" Carrouso cried. "Nicole's coming back!"

"You must see this!" Goldblum shouted.

"She's awake?" Toby asked, entering the room with Sam, Glenda and Harry.

"We must see this!" Sam cried out.

"Are you serious?" Glenda asked.

"Our dear niece," Harry said.

"Give Timlook PD a call!" Glenda said. "And forward the message to Dave and Jim."

"I'll call them!" Toby cried. "On Nicole's mobile."

"Nicole, Nicole," Carrouso said gently. "It's us!"

"Where am I?" Nicole asked, her voice breaking. She opened her eyes. "Where is Dave? Where are Dave and Jim? Toby?" Tears trickled down her mature face, her eyes big and her teeth clenched gently.

"It's us!" Goldblum exclaimed, his bearded face grinning as he parted his long brown hair. "We're all alive! And Dave and Jim are alive and in Timlook. Toby's calling Timlook PD now."

"We thought you'd never make it!" Carrouso said.

"But you must rest," Glen said. "You're one damn lucky girl, Nicole."

Nicole chuckled, a sly grin revealing her shining white teeth.

"You can't get rid of me that easily, guys," she whispered.

Sam chuckled too.

"You bet we can't," he laughed. "Toby's returning with your mobile."

"I called Timlook PD, Nicole," Toby explained. "But Dave and Jim weren't present. They're hiding out at Dale and Melissa's farmstead with the other detectives, so Captain Merson gave me the number there and I gave them a call. Dave answered."

Toby passed the phone over to Nicole, and she pulled herself up, crossed her legs and put it to her ear.

"Hi, Dave, honey," she began, her voice still quite weak.

"You're alive!" Dave exclaimed. "I thought I'd never see you again."

"I remember the shootout outside the Christian church in Chicago," Nicole began. "And catching a rifle bullet in my chest, then I blacked out.

"I remember the afterlife, floating in a white mist between my earthly body and the world called heaven. I met the ghost of my mother. We talked, and she was full of wisdom. She returned to heaven, but my ghost wasn't ready to go there. I was trapped. But I reckon I'm not ready for the afterworld."

"You reckon, right," Dave said. "The afterlife is not ready for you. I've missed you."

"I bet you have," Nicole agreed playfully.

"I can't wait for you to return to Timlook," Dave added. "In the meantime, the six of us are at Dale and Melissa's farmstead with Kanaris's guys, and we'll shortly be joined by three FBI Agents. Cortez, Pazerra and their six bodyguards, as well as the Mck-Fee brothers and their mob, are still at large. Both gangs are probably in Pennsylvania, in Timlook itself. It feels like we may never escape the nightmare of the New England Net."

"Juan Pazerra will never give up until his mob have massacred Sam Ringwood's men," Nicole pointed out, her voice growing stronger. "And Matt and Ray Mck-Fee won't rest until they murder all six of you. Watch your backs, detectives. Especially you, Dave. I didn't return to this world just to lose my husband and my friends. Be careful."

"We will," Dave said. "Jim wants to talk to you and Sam."

"How are you, young lady?" Jim said with a chuckle.

"I'm okay, Jim," Nicole reassured the bearded New Yorker. "But I need plenty of rest. Sam wants to talk to you."

"Bring him on," Jim said lightly.

"Hi Jim, it's me," Sam said.

"You're still alive after the attack," Jim observed.

"We made mincemeat of those guys," Sam said proudly. "Toby protected Nicole with one of my handguns and terminated Vaston and Lumumber single-handedly. Then we called the Chicago police. How did you know about that mob attack? And why didn't you call to warn us?"

"It's a long story, Sam," Jim explained. "We ran into the Mck-Fees at a saloon outside Akron in Ohio, and they told us how they had ferreted through the telephone directories covering Illinois and Pennsylvania and found only one address with the name Lamenski. That's how they located their country estate. They told us they would send their mob under Vaston and Lumumber to hit the place. Dave tried to warn you by calling Nicole's mobile, but it was switched off. You wouldn't believe how scared we were."

"That figures," Sam said. "I heard how all the drug cartels have been busted in a series of sting operations. We watched the Chicago News on TV. We also heard how the De Francos and their mob were found dead outside a burned-out limousine a few miles from Chicago, and that the De Marcos, John Hazinski, Miles Carter and nine Mexicans were found dead, shot by your people at their hideout in Pittsburgh."

"It was in Pittsburgh that we confiscated an incriminating file," Jim told Sam. "Or, I found the file after we took down the De Marcos and their thugs. In this file was the whole list of cartels in the New England Net, their crooked deals and hit operations. We took the train to Timlook and passed the file over to Captain Merson at the department, who emailed the info to all the police departments from Chicago to Boston. They then pulled a series of sting operations against the cartel addresses.

"The New York police busted the Cortez-Pazerra Cartel building, but Cortez, Pazerra and their bodyguards escaped. Richard Kanaris's vice squad and the FBI pulled an operation against Jack Fallon's cartel in Timlook, but two thugs gave them the slip. The Mck-Fee brothers and their mob remain at large, but Kanaris informed us that his detectives will force Fallon to arrange a meeting with the Mck-Fees, and then they will nail the mob."

"I have to give it to you and Dave," Sam said with a laugh, "you two really know how to get results. Thanks to you, Dave and Captain Merson, we found the drug lords' Achilles' heel, and the information on that file will lead to the destruction of the New England Net.

"But we can't relax knowing Cortez, Pazerra and the Mck-Fees are still out there with personal vendettas against us and your people. They will unite their mobs. It ain't over until it's over, pal."

"Well, I'm glad everybody at your end is still breathing," Jim told him. "But all my people can do now is lie low. And the same with you, the Lamenskis and your brave son, Toby.

"I must break off the call now, Dale and Melissa won't thank me for running up their telephone bill. Good day, Ringwood."

"Good day, Mitchell," Sam replied. "And it's not Dale and Melissa's bill. Toby called using Nicole's mobile phone; it's her bill we're running up! Have a nice day."

"Have a nice day," Jim finished off.

They broke off the call, and as Jim replaced the receiver, Sam switched off Nicole's mobile and passed it to her.

"Put it on the dressing table, please," Nicole said.

"Okay, sister," Sam said. "You get plenty of rest."

"We're glad you're back with us," Toby enthused.

Nicole smiled at him, then towards Harry and Glenda. She could hear the CSI and Forensics people talking downstairs, and felt that it was a warm, sunny day outside. She could see the trees displaying their red, brown and green foliage, and the lawn's lush grass growing a foot long, and was very happy to be alive.

***

At the farmstead, Dave, Jim and Dale were eating at the dinner table opposite Melissa,

Reynolds and Bernardo, while Kanaris's men consumed their meals on the two armchairs and the settee. All eleven detectives were dining on platefuls of beef lasagna with French fries and green vegetables. The male Homicide detectives were dressed in jeans and casual shirts and Melissa wore a medium-length green skirt, a blue T-shirt and a black sweater over the top. Kanaris's vice cops were also casually dressed.

"You enjoying the lunch?" Dale asked everybody.

"You'd better be," Melissa insisted gently. "I went through a lot of work to cook this lasagna."

"It's the works," Reynolds reassured her.

"It could do with more salt," Bernardo said, while spooning in another large mouthful.

"And pepper too," Dave said with a wink. "But you've really pulled no punches with the herbs."

"Hey lady," Jim added. "It's great lasagna. And great fries and veg. Sorry, they get like this sometimes."

"The lasagna and veg are cool," Dale said, smiling at his wife.

Melissa grinned, her teeth shining between her plain lips. She shook her black hair back behind her narrow shoulders.

"You bet they're cool," she said playfully. "If not, you can cook next time. How about you vice cops?"

"Not enough salt," Kanaris joined in.

"Not enough pepper," Jan added lightly.

"There's plenty of pepper," Felt said, trying to hold back a laugh.

"But the taste is overpowered by the herbs," Felder said sarcastically.

"And spices," Blondel added, dramatically pushing away his plate. "Too much paprika and cayenne pepper."

"There's more than enough pepper then!" Dave said, winking again. "I'm more into the beef's taste."

"Okay, okay, guys," Melissa objected shyly.

"No, really, it's the works," Dave assured her. "The best lasagna I've ever had."

"You're right, it's top class." Jim agreed.

"And it's good enough for me," Dale praised her.

At that moment, the doorbell rang.

"That's the front door," Dale continued. "You want me to answer it?"

"I'll answer it," Melissa decided.

She pulled her handgun out of her purse, approached the hallway and eased open the door, which was secured by a chain. She aimed her weapon through the gap in the doorway. Dave, Jim and Dale were behind her, also readying their handguns.

"Who is it?" Melissa asked.

"It's the FBI," the leading man reassured her. "I'm Federal Agent Neil Green. These two are Agents Liam White and Tim Nelson."

"Show us your ID," Dale demanded.

"Done," Green said.

They passed the ID cards through the gap in the doorway, and Dave and Jim examined one card while Dale and Melissa studied the other two.

"You can come in," Melissa said. She released the chain, yanked open the door and welcomed in the three Feds, all of whom were bearded men dressed in black suits. "Make yourselves at home, guys."

"We have no lunch for you," Dale informed them. "But we have juices, lemonade and coffee."

"We're okay," Green told him. "We all had drinks before we left our department."

"We've eaten," Jim said. "And Kanaris's men must go and conduct an interrogation."

"You want to leave us, guys?" Dave asked the vice cops.

"We will," Kanaris agreed.

"Let's roll," Blondel decided.

The vice cops moved towards their squad van and climbed inside. Kanaris made a U-turn, accelerated through the farmstead's exit and rode along the highway leading towards Timlook.

***

The Mck-Fees' van sped towards a building site in North Timlook, a mile from Jack Fallon's former cartel building in Warsaw Street, while Jose Cortez's helicopter descended upon the same location.

Matt and Ray climbed out of their vehicle and Cortez, Pazerra and their six long-haired bodyguards switched off the helicopter's engine, so the rotor slowed to an abrupt stop, and then got out. The three mustached Mexicans, three bearded Cubans and two Americans approached Matt and Ray Mck-Fee, all eight brandishing rifles.

"You've fled New York," Matt said.

"How was the journey?" Ray inquired.

"A long journey, my friends," Cortez told them. "But now the manpower of your mob has increased by eight men."

"That makes seventeen of us against six cops," Pazerra added. "More if you count Jack Fallon and his thugs."

"Fallon's cartel has been busted," Matt said. "But two men escaped, and then gave me a call. They have their own plan to deal with Bradley, Mitchell and the other detectives by infiltrating their location using false IDs.

"We'll attack Morgan's farmstead from the outside. It's ten miles south of Timlook with only one highway leading towards it. By my watch, it's four p.m. You guys get into our vehicle and we'll drive there together. We'll be there in just over an hour, a few minutes after five. Let's jump to it, guys."

Matt and Ray doubled back towards the van with Cortez, Pazerra and their bodyguards walking behind, and as the Mck-Fees leapt into the front seats, Cortez's gang were ushered through the rear doors and into the main compartment by the seven thugs already in there.

In an hour's time, both mobs would execute a ferocious and bloody massacre to finish off Dave's detectives for good.

***

The doorbell of Melissa's farmhouse rang loudly again, and Dave, Jim and Dale approached the front door with Melissa and the three FBI Agents following them, all seven focusing their handguns towards the door. Dale unfastened the lock, left the chain in place and pulled the door ajar.

"Who is it?" he wanted to know.

"We're FBI," one man replied.

Unlike the bearded Federal Agents already inside the farmhouse, the two men in black suits were clean-shaven.

"Identify yourselves," Jim demanded. "Nobody told us you were coming."

"Your ID cards will clear you," Dave explained.

"And your names," Melissa ordered.

"Agents Neil Marvin and Welman North," the first man announced. "Here's our ID."

They displayed their cards through the doorway's gap. The Homicide Detectives had no reason to doubt Agents Marvin and North, but still hesitated.

"Shall we let them in?" Dale asked Agent Green.

"Their ID is genuine," Green said.

"Let them in," Jim decided.

Dale unfastened the chain, pulled open the door and Marvin and North entered.

Dave harbored suspicions about the men, for Jim had rightly pointed out that nobody had phoned to inform them they were coming.

"Why did you come over unannounced?" he asked.

"You never phoned us," Jim said.

"Explain yourselves," Melissa demanded.

"We're from the FBI's Washington DC branch," North told them.

"You came all the way from Washington DC?" Dave snapped.

"You mind if we see your ID cards again?" Green blurted.

"Okay, go ahead," Marvin said, pulling out his ID a second time. "But our mobiles have run out of credit, so you mind if we use your telephone upstairs, Manuchi, Morgan? We'll phone the Washington DC branch to confirm we're who we say we are."

"Go ahead," Melissa agreed. "Green, White and Nelson, you'll watch them. Go upstairs with them."

"Watch them closely," Dale ordered.

The Feds ascended the stairs and covered the distance towards Dale and Melissa's bedroom.

"You thinking what I'm thinking?" Jim asked.

"I have a really bad feeling about this," Dave said.

"I don't like it either," Jim commented.

"You mind if I use your downstairs telephone to overhear Marvin's call?" Dave asked Melissa. "They claimed their mobiles had run out of credit. They don't want us to contact the branch. I really don't like this."

"More to the point, I never saw the branch's telephone number on their ID cards," Jim claimed. "Did you, Dale?"

"I can't say I did," Dale replied.

"Yeah, use my downstairs phone and listen in," Melissa decided.

Jim yanked the receiver off the hook and listened for a moment.

"I hear no bleeping from the upstairs phone," Jim said.

"They haven't touched the phone," Melissa snapped. "I knew all along they were dirty."

"I hear arguing upstairs," Dave told her.

***

Green, White and Nelson examined the ID cards of Marvin and North.

"There's no telephone number on each card!" Green exclaimed. "And the branch's address is false. I once visited the DC branch, and it wasn't on Warsaw Street."

Marvin and North produced their handguns from their jacket pockets. Marvin fired three shots into Nelson, and North pumped two into White.

"What are you doing?" Green yelled.

But before he could shout for help, Marvin and North released three gunshots into him. He fell to the floor with a sickening thud and lay beside the other two Feds.

***

The detectives downstairs overheard the shouting in Dale and Melissa's room, eight muffled gunshots and then three bodies thudding to the floor, the noise vibrating through the ceiling. Jim had replaced the receiver, but two minutes later the downstairs telephone rang, and he grabbed it again.

"Hello, who is it?" Jim demanded. "I'm Detective Sergeant James Mitchell answering from the farmstead of Detectives Dale Manuchi and Melissa Morgan. Who's calling?"

"It's me, Richard Kanaris," the bearded hippy replied, his voice frantic. "We've finished giving Jack Fallon a ruthless interrogation."

"Go on," Jim insisted.

***

On the highway leading towards the Manuchi farmstead, hidden from the farmhouse's front door and windows by a distance of over five hundred yards, the Mck-Fees' van came to a halt. Matt turned off the ignition before he and Ray shoved open the front doors, jumped outside, slammed the doors shut and approached the rear. Turning his own key, Matt pulled open the rear doors. The first to leap outside were Cortez, Pazerra and their men.

"All eight of us will lie in wait in the farmhouse's front yard to cut off the cops' escape," Cortez snarled.

"Me and Ray will wait round the back yard, in case they attempt an exit through the back doors," Matt hissed.

"Jack Fallon's two phony FBI agents will have wasted the three Feds backing up Bradley and Mitchell by now," Ray sneered. "You guys backing up Matt and myself will storm into the farmhouse and engage Bradley's people."

"Remember, Melissa Morgan is our business," Matt ordered. "It was our big brother James who she killed, and I'll enjoy pumping lead into the dumb bitch."

Cortez, Pazerra and their six bodyguards held their high-velocity rifles under their muscular arms, while the Mck-Fees and their seven thugs grabbed their terrifying weaponry and then closed the rear doors with a ferocious clanging sound.

"Us guys are about to make history," Ray said.

"Let's give these motherfuckers a taste of their own medicine," Matt sneered.

The seventeen heavily armed thugs advanced slowly down the highway until they reached the farmstead's entrance, then split up.

***

Jim was becoming more terrified as Kanaris told him the information the vice cops had extracted from Jack Fallon.

"Those two men who escaped from Fallon's hideout," Kanaris began, "are Neil Marvin and Welman North. Before the Mck-Fees arrived in Timlook, Fallon bleeped Matt Mck-Fee on his mobile to tell him Marvin and North would pose as FBI Agents with fake IDs. They would infiltrate Melissa's farmhouse and waste Agents Neil Green, Liam White and Tim Nelson.

"If Marvin and North come to the farmhouse door, don't let them in. The Mck-Fees, Jose Cortez, Juan Pazerra and their two mobs are about to pull a hit against you. Me and my men will run ourselves over to the farmstead now. I repeat, don't let Marvin and North in."

"It's too late, they're already here," Jim snapped. He bashed the receiver down and then turned to Dave, Dale and Melissa. "You were right, Melissa, they're dirty."

"They came over with no notice, there were no telephone numbers on their ID cards and the address was false," Dave remarked, his eyes and face serious. "Warsaw Street is in North Timlook, not Washington DC."

"That figures," Dale commented.

"And the only way they'd think of that name is because they're from Jack Fallon's cartel building in Warsaw Street," Melissa explained.

"They're working for Jack Fallon," Dave said. "Or they were."

Clenching their handguns, the detectives vacated the hallway and rejoined Reynolds and Bernardo in the dining room, who had removed their guns from their holsters.

"We overheard you whispering," Reynolds said.

"This is going to turn messy," Bernardo snarled.

"You're damn right it is," Dave growled.

At that moment, Agents Marvin and North descended the stairs and approached the detectives. Melissa walked up to Marvin, seized the lapels of his jacket and, with violent force, smashed her knee into his crotch. Marvin screamed with terrible agony before Dale punched him twice in the kidneys, flooring him. North reached for his handgun, but Dave swung two blows into his stomach then exploded his fist into North's face. Jim followed up with two more punches, which bloodied North's mouth and sent him hurtling to the floor. As Reynolds and Bernardo covered the detectives, their guns aimed towards the false Feds, Jim forcefully restrained North while Dave fastened handcuffs onto his wrists, pinning his arms behind his back, and Melissa thrust an armlock on Marvin as Dale handcuffed him.

"What is the meaning of this?" Marvin blurted.

"Please don't kill us!" North wailed.

"That's less than you deserve, you despicable shit!" Melissa shouted.

"You worked for Jack Fallon!" Dave snapped. "You're not too bright are you!"

"Where are Matt and Ray Mck-Fee?" Jim cried. "Where are the Mck-Fees? You arseholes!"

Dave and Jim prodded their handguns into North's kidneys, while Melissa jabbed her weapon into the back of Marvin's head.

"We don't have all day!" Dale yelled.

"I'm about to pull the trigger!" Melissa threatened Marvin.

"No, no!" Marvin screamed. "Please don't kill us! You'll regret this! I'm fucking telling you, Morgan!"

"The Mck-Fees and their men are here!" Dave called, having spotted them through the window advancing towards the house. "We must gag Marvin and North and knock them out!"

"No jerking about!" Melissa cried.

"Here are the gags!" Dale shouted.

He thrust one gag into Marvin's mouth and tied it behind his head, while Jim forced the other into North's mouth and secured it with a knot.

The detectives wrenched Marvin and North off the floor, and as Dave hurled two punches into Marvin's face, Dale used the butt of his handgun and swung a hard blow to his head to knock him unconscious. Marvin was out cold in the next second. Melissa smashed North's head twice, swinging her handgun violently and knocking him out as well, and then Dave and Jim dragged both men out of the dining room, through the hallway and into the kitchen.

"We must act fast," Jim snapped frantically. "Reynolds and Bernardo, you two hide in the bathroom upstairs. Dale, Melissa, you hide in your bedroom, as it's opposite the bathroom, and all of you will catch the mobsters in the crossfire as they walk up the hallway. Dave and me will hide behind those curtains in the conservatory the other side of the kitchen and take the remaining thugs by surprise. Now, go."

Dave and Jim moved from the kitchen to the conservatory and hid behind the curtains flanking the room's pane of glass so that any mobsters in the backyard would fail to spot them, while Dale led the other three detectives upstairs.

Dave and Jim waited and waited, and this waiting was terrible. Tension ground at their nerves, bodies and minds as they both stood completely silent, tightening their hands around their handguns. Sweat streamed down their faces and palms as they fingered the triggers.

Marvin and North were coming round, and Dave muttered the words, "Damn it!" His nerves jarred violently as he heard the brutal voices of three Mexicans, three Cubans and two Americans whispering outside the front door, passing orders to seven other Americans. Then, one of the thugs smashed their bodyweight against the front door. The door crashed open violently and the four black men and three white guys stormed into the house.

"Where are they?" the white-haired man whispered.

"They're hiding," the bearded guy said.

"We'll split up," one of the black men muttered. "Us four will search the dining room, the bathroom and the bedrooms, while you three search the kitchen and conservatory. The Mck-Fees are round the back."

The black guys burst into the dining room, aiming their rifles. The white men flicked on the kitchen light and saw Marvin and North lying handcuffed and gagged on the floor. The phony FBI agents were muffling angrily through the gags.

"You two failed us," the white-haired man growled coldly. "You will die."

Two of the thugs sent a couple of deafening shots into Marvin and North and they slumped on the floor. They then took menacing glances into the conservatory and searched the open room for half a minute. The Mck-Fee brothers beckoned them from the farmyard.

"They're not here," the bearded man snarled.

The men returned to the kitchen, turning their backs to the curtains, and Dave and Jim picked their critical moment. Dave aimed his handgun and fired a single shot into one man's head, causing the other two guys to spin round with rage and ferocity. Dave blasted a second man in the face with two shots, who then fell helplessly to the floor, while Jim's weapon vomited two bullets into the third man's head.

Both cops scrambled out from behind the curtains and darted through the conservatory and into the kitchen before diving to the floor. Two of the black men in the dining room had stormed violently through the hallway and saw the kitchen containing five dead bodies, and Dave and Jim lying on their fronts.

The black guys took aim with their rifles, but Dave and Jim pre-empted with two spurts of gunfire from their handguns. Dave cut down one guy with three savage blasts, and the man fell just as Jim brought down the other, killing him with four deafening shots. Both thugs were splayed across the floor amongst the five bodies already there.

Jim and Dave scrambled through the kitchen and the hallway, slammed the front door shut to prevent the remaining eight mobsters from getting in and then dived into the lounge room and behind the settee.

Two black mobsters on the upstairs landing were engaged in a savage shootout with Dale and Melissa. Melissa blazed with four shots and Dale fired seven, but the thugs leaned against the wall to avoid being hit. Dale and Melissa retreated backwards until they were behind the double bed, and the thugs pinned them there with a vicious and deafening hail of rifle fire. Dave and Jim shot at the mobsters from the living room, but missed, but then Reynolds and Bernardo fired from the bathroom. Bernardo cut one man down with three shots before he retreated behind the doorway, and as the other black guy spun round and took aim at him, Reynolds emerged from the other side of the doorway and fired four shots, killing the mobster instantly.

Dale, Melissa, Reynolds and Bernardo emerged from both rooms and raced downstairs to rejoin Dave and Jim.

"Thanks, Reynolds, Bernardo," Melissa enthused.

"You got those two off our backs," Dale added.

"Let's check through the front window," Jim growled.

The detectives crawled towards the windowsill and glanced outside. They ducked as the remaining eight thugs smashed the window to smithereens with several ferocious blasts of their rifles and crawled backwards to hide behind the settee.

"I have an idea," Dave whispered to the others. "Dale and me will draw the Mck-Fees away from the farmyard. You four keep these eight guys tied up in a shootout."

"We understand," Jim responded.

"Away we go," Dale said.

Dave and Dale fled into the hallway, and then raced through the kitchen and pulled open the back door. They instantly retreated as the Mck-Fee brothers sent several rifle shots towards them from behind one of the two barns. As they pulled back to reload, Dave and Dale seized two rifles from the kitchen floor carnage, hurried outside and fired three times each at the barn. They sped across the yard, while the Mck-Fees fired savagely at them, and took cover inside the west barn.

The Mck-Fees followed the detectives across the yard and entered the barn. They failed to spot either Dave or Dale, and Matt suggested that he and Ray split up. Matt made his way right to search the old cattle bays, and Ray headed left and then turned right, towards a mass of haystacks in an empty cattle enclosure.

Dave and Dale were hiding behind two cattle troughs on either side of Ray.

"Over here," Dale yelled, and he sent a deafening blast from his rifle into Ray's shoulder.

Dave then pumped two exploding shots into Ray's back, and the mobster hurtled to the ground, his torso plastered with blood. Then Dale made a fatal mistake. He ventured out from behind the cattle trough to ensure Ray was dead, exposing himself to further danger.

Matt came from just around the corner, aimed his rifle at Dale and, with a deafening gunshot, sent a large fiery-hot bullet into Dale's shoulder, the impact throwing Dale forwards so the young detective plummeted to the ground, losing his grip on the rifle. Dale instantly rolled onto his back. Matt sprinted across the enclosure and, as Dale was being tortured by the burning agony in his shoulder, Matt kicked him in the head, knocking him out cold.

Dave aimed his rifle at Matt, but the gun jammed and he had to react fast. He charged towards Matt's midriff and both men crashed against the wall. Dave dropped his own rifle on impact, so the two of them fought violently over Matt's weapon. Dave pinned Matt against the wall, but Matt's sheer rage and adrenalin gave him the strength of ten men. He forced Dave round and trapped him against the wall with the rifle wedged against his throat. Matt smashed his forehead into Dave's face, but Dave had instinctively turned his head and only suffered a laceration near his eye. Then Matt sent his knee crunching into Dave's crotch, so the young Quaker screamed in agony and doubled up, only to receive five deadly punches in the face, lacerating his nose and fracturing his jaw. Blood streamed from Dave's nostrils and mouth, and he fell to the ground. He tried to grab his own handgun inside the pocket of his jeans, but Matt kicked at his arm, fracturing the elbow and sending the handgun flying from his hands. Dave screamed out with hellish pain, and then Matt finished him off with three kicks into his stomach.

Dave was curled up on the ground, his arms and knees around his stomach and crotch, totally defenseless. Matt reached for his rifle and aimed at the young cop.

"It's over, Bradley," Matt snarled. "You should never have crossed me. You're going to die, and then I'll kill Manuchi."

"Drop your weapon, Mck-Fee!" Melissa shouted sternly from across the barn. "Or you will die!"

Melissa was standing at the enclosure's entrance, aiming her handgun at Matt's back. Matt hesitated, then he spun round and raised his rifle, but Melissa squeezed the trigger. She pumped three roaring shots into Matt's chest, killing him in the space of three seconds, and he tumbled to the earthen floor.

Melissa ran frantically towards Dave and Dale, as they lay close together, critically injured on the ground, Dale regaining consciousness.

"Dave! Dale!" Melissa screamed. "Oh shit!" She lay Dave on his back as he was writhing in agony and then reached out to her husband's shoulder, putting pressure on the bleeding gunshot wound.

***

The remaining mobsters, including Jose Cortez and Juan Pazerra, continued firing at the farmhouse's front window until they were running low on ammunition. There were eight of them against the three cops inside the house, but then Jim's group were relieved to see Richard Kanaris's vice squad speeding through the farmstead's entrance in their van.

The five bearded detectives got out of the vehicle and started firing at the thugs from behind. Jan, Felt and Felder cut down two Mexicans with a hail of gunfire, while Kanaris and Blondel killed the two Americans with seven blasts of their handguns.

Jim leapt up from behind the settee and aimed his gun towards Cortez, blazing with two vicious blasts so the Mexican fell, making five thugs lying on the ground with rivers of blood spilling from their wounds.

The three Cubans, including Pazerra, forced their weight against the house's front door to avoid Kanaris's men. They smashed the door off its hinges and stormed into the dining room, but Jim, Reynolds and Bernardo were ready for them. Reynolds and Bernardo brought down two men with five shots between them, while Jim sent three shots into Pazerra. The drug lord hit the wall and slumped onto the floor, the blood gushing from his wounds smearing the wall and floor dark red.

"Call an ambulance," Jim told Reynolds and Bernardo. "I'll check on Dave, Dale and Melissa."

***

Melissa placed Dave's fractured arm in a sling.

"Take care of Dale first," Dave said, his intentions noble. "He's worse off than I am."

Dale's arm was now numbed by agony.

"Thanks, Melissa, you saved our lives," Dale muttered painfully. "We owe you one."

"Saving our lives is becoming a habit with you," Dave added with a smile of respect. "You got Mck-Fee off my back. Thanks again."

"It's my pleasure," Melissa said, grinning.

She kissed Dave on the cheek and then gave Dale a gentle, soothing kiss on the mouth. The kiss relaxed Dale and he lost consciousness in the next ten seconds. She caressed his forehead as Jim came into the barn and hurried towards them.

"Jesus Christ!" Jim exclaimed. "What madness! We've called an ambulance, Melissa."

"Good on you, Jim," Melissa said.

Jim patted the young woman on the back for her bravery in confronting Matt Mck-Fee and saving the lives of two men. They both smiled with joy. At that moment, they heard the high whine of an ambulance and a few squad cars racing down the highway and fanning out into the farmstead.

"I hear Captain Merson addressing the uniforms," Dave commented.

***

At Miami PD, Chief Kavubu had just received a phone call from Captain Merson. The chief replaced the receiver and addressed Captain Olmera.

"I have some news."

"Some news, Chief?" Olmera asked.

"The Mck-Fee brothers are dead," Kavubu told him. "They were shot and killed by Detectives Dave Bradley, Dale Manuchi and Melissa Morgan in a foiled hit operation. Their gang were killed in the shootout on Detective Morgan's farmstead outside Timlook. Jose Cortez, Juan Pazerra and their six bodyguards were also killed. The drug cartels are no more."

"You want me to pass on the news to our people?" Olmera wanted to know.

"Do it, Captain," Kavubu ordered.

He rose from his seat and he and Olmera vacated his office and entered the main office to address

DA Michael Turillo and the teams of uniforms and vice cops.

"We have news you'll want to hear," Olmera said.

"We're dying to hear this," Turillo replied.

"The network of drug cartels known as the New England Net has been smashed," Olmera continued. "Only two gangs were left, the Cortez-Pazerra mob and the Mck-Fees, and both were terminated on a farmstead outside Timlook by six Homicide detectives and a team of vice cops. Jose Cortez, Juan Pazerra and the Mck-Fee brothers were all killed. All six Homicide detectives, including Dave Bradley, James Mitchell, Dale Manuchi and Melissa Morgan, survived the hit operation.

"And Detective Nicole Lamenski has recovered from her critical condition at a secret estate outside Chicago and is ready for Detectives Sam Ringwood, Rico Carrouso, Martin Goldblum and Glen Hawke to drop her at Timlook Airport on their way back to Miami. Sam's son Toby Ringwood will also return to Florida."

There was a chorus of cheers and jubilation from the uniforms and vice cops on hearing that Sam's vice cops and Dave's Homicide detectives had survived the nightmare inflicted by the New England Net.

Squad Leaders Jack Trogan, Jim Curry and Bruce Dwane approached Chief Kavubu and Captain Olmera, accompanied by Detectives Philo Magee, Enrique Rogers and Rogers's four hippy cops.

"The FBI plane is ready at Miami Airport," Trogan told them.

"It was filled with fuel yesterday," Curry explained.

"And it's been on standby ever since," Dwane added.

"We're ready to take the flight to Chicago, pick up Sam's people and Nicole Lamenski, fly to Timlook and drop Nicole at the airport to meet with Dave Bradley and James Mitchell," Magee announced.

"All we're doing now is awaiting your orders, Chief, Captain, DA Turillo," Rogers told all three.

"You must take the flight now," Kavubu said. "Accompanying you will be four FBI agents, three men and a woman. The best of luck."

"The same from me," Olmera concluded. "The best of luck."

"And me too," DA Turillo added.

"Thanks, we'll be on our way," Curry replied.

***

On the afternoon of the following day, the FBI plane touched down at Timlook Airport, where Dave and Jim were waiting for Nicole in the airport terminal. Nicole walked down the corridor, flanked by Sam and Toby, with Carrouso, Goldblum and Glen following behind.

"Hi there," Dave cheered.

"How are you guys doing?" Jim asked.

"Pretty good," Sam enthused.

"Nicole's made a remarkable recovery," Toby pointed out.

"You bet I have," Nicole told them.

Dave and Nicole embraced each other, and their mouths met in a gentle kiss. Then Nicole approached Toby and her lips met his cheek.

"Thank you for saving my life when Vaston and Lumumber tried to kill me in my sleep," she said. "I'll always have a place in my heart for you, but I'm glad to be back with Dave."

"I can live with that," Toby commented. "Saving your life was no problem. I would do the same thing again."

"I know you would," Nicole remarked.

"There's other women down in Florida you can date, Toby," Carrouso said.

"Women in bikinis on the beach," Goldblum said.

"One day, you'll find a woman you're suited to," Glen advised the young lawyer.

"But let me guess," Sam said. "Not the spitting image of your mother or sister."

"No, Dad," Toby said.

"One day, we should take a trip to Miami and see you," Dave decided. "Jim, myself and Nicole."

"If that's what you want," Carrouso agreed.

"Why not, guys?" Sam said.

"I'm all for it," Jim said.

Toby paused, and Dave read the serious thought in his mind.

"I pray we never go through another nightmare similar to the New England Net," Toby told him.

"Never again," Dave replied. "We took on the second Mck-Fee Cartel and its network of drug cartels. And your dad's people, my people and

Richard Kanaris's vice cops, we worked together and supported each other through thick and thin. We took them on and we won."

"We beat the Mck-Fees in the end," Sam praised everybody. "But however many criminals and drug dealers we put away or kill, there's always more to replace them."

"It is a sad reality," Toby indicated. "Even though a great deal has been achieved with America's zero-tolerance policy against all levels of crime, the law must cooperate with families in our communities and tackle poverty and deprivation at the grass-roots level. Only then will we destroy the incentive for the supply and demand of drugs."

"That's exactly my thinking," Dave pointed out. "By tackling poverty, deprivation and lack of discipline in families and in schools, we'll not only eradicate drug trafficking, we'll eradicate all types of crime.

"President George Bush did nothing to tackle our social problems, but the Democrats under Barack Obama have given us Americans a new beginning and a new future. Good luck to Obama."

"Good luck to the world," Jim enthused, a sharp grin reaching his beard.

"And good luck to Law and Order," Dave added lightly.

At that moment, Trogan, Curry, Dwane, Magee, Rogers and the four bearded hippy cops came down the terminal with the four FBI agents walking behind them. The two Feds in their forties, a black guy and a white man were dressed in suits, while the other two were in their late thirties, a man with dark hair and a mature-looking woman with light brown hair, and were wearing FBI uniforms.

The vice cops and the FBI people halted, and Sam and Toby greeted them again, ready to continue the journey down to Florida.

"We're sorry to keep you guys waiting," Sam remarked.

"You'd better make your move," Jim suggested.

"But we'll see you again," Nicole decided.

"Have a good return flight to Florida," Dave said.

"We will," Sam said. "Farewell, you guys."

"Goodbye, Dave, Jim, Nicole," Toby told them.

"Goodbye, guys," Dave replied.

Sam and Toby followed the vice cops and the FBI people towards the plane on the runway, with Carrouso, Goldblum and Glen walking behind them. All eighteen passengers vacated the airport terminal and headed outside.

Dave, Jim and Nicole watched them board the plane, and then made their way back through the airport terminal, and then outside. Nicole's mouth met Dave's face with a gentle kiss.

***

At Melissa's farmstead, the front door and window had been replaced, and Dale and Melissa had prepared a banquet to celebrate the detectives' victory over the drug cartels. It was lunchtime, and Dale, Melissa, Reynolds and Bernardo offered their final gratitude to Kanaris, Jan, Felt, Felder and Blondel for driving to their rescue. Kanaris's vice squad had to leave before the banquet was set out on the dining table, but the Homicide detectives were not offended.

"We must head back to work now," Kanaris told Dale and Melissa. "How about you save us some food and bring it to the police department? We're really tied up at the moment."

"Don't worry, Richard," Melissa reassured him, her face grinning. "Don't feel guilty. Your vice squad played their part in protecting this place from Mck-Fee's men, intervening at the last minute."

"Melissa's taking a day off tomorrow, but I'll bring some food in for you, Captain Merson and all the cops at Timlook PD," Dale promised. "That includes your vice squad. We have three times as much food over here as we need, so help yourselves at any time. You've earned it."

Kanaris and his team thanked Dale and Melissa and then bade farewell to the young couple.

"Goodbye, Kanaris," Reynolds added, his face lit up with a beaming smile. "We'll see you again, guys."

"See you again, señors," Bernardo added.

"Same to you all, pals," Kanaris replied gently.

The vice squad vacated the farmhouse and made their way towards their van.

Bernardo rubbed his mustache thoughtfully. Reynolds and Bernardo felt better for having had a shave, and they patted each other on the back before glancing towards Dale and Melissa.

"How's your arm now, Dale?" Reynolds asked. "You sure took a bullet for Dave."

"My arm's mended now," Dale replied, smiling with joy. "Dave took worse punishment from Matt Mck-Fee than I did, but he's also recovered. He and Jim have driven to the airport to pick up Nicole. We both owe our lives to Melissa."

"Don't thank me, honey," Melissa insisted, a grin touching her feminine face. "It's my job. I owe more to you, and even more to Dave and Jim."

"We all pulled through, honey," Dale said. "We all made it."

"I'm relieved Dave's recovered," Melissa told Dale. "Our skill with firearms saved the day."

"The feeling is mutual," Dale decided. "I think Dave, Jim and Nicole are back from the airport. That's them now. Reynolds, Bernardo, can you get the food out of the oven?"

"Sure we can," they replied.

Dale and Melissa approached the front door and pulled it open to greet Dave, Jim and Nicole.

"Hi there," Nicole greeted them. "We saw Kanaris's guys leaving. I guess they couldn't stay."

"I'm afraid not," Dale said with a chuckle.

"I'm as hungry as a lion!" Jim laughed. "Is the food ready?"

"It's ready," Melissa replied.

"Then let us all boldly make our way in," Dave decided, grinning joyfully across his boyish face. "Do you all want help with the preparations?"

They entered the farmhouse and lowered themselves into the armchairs. The outlook for them now was a positive one.

AUTHOR PROFILE

Michael Elia was born in Southampton in 1968. He was educated at Bartholomew School near Oxford. He has autism and Tourette's Syndrome, and lives in accommodation for people with autism in Maidenhead. He has also written A Trio of Cartels, Web of Crime, Nature's Revenge, Fear of the Unknown and Claws of Fear.

Publisher Information

Rowanvale Books provides publishing services to independent authors, writers and poets all over the globe. We deliver a personal, honest and efficient service that allows authors to see their work published, while remaining in control of the process and retaining their creativity. By making publishing services available to authors in a cost-effective and ethical way, we at Rowanvale Books hope to ensure that the local, national and international community benefits from a steady stream of good quality literature.

For more information about us, our authors or our publications, please get in touch.

www.rowanvalebooks.com
info@rowanvalebooks.com

What Did You Think of The New England Net?

A big thank you for purchasing this book. It means a lot that you chose this book specifically from such a wide range on offer. I do hope you enjoyed it.

Book reviews are incredibly important for an author. All feedback helps them improve their writing for future projects and for developing this edition. If you are able to spare a few minutes to post a review on Amazon, that would be much appreciated.